The Strolling Players

Let us join for a space a company of strolling players, and with them become enchanted with the world of make-believe in the isolated communities of the Highlands of Scotland.

To this magical land comes Jonathan Harley, the famous actor, already very nearly spoilt by the applause of the adoring diamond audiences. Many people travel through life and miss the shadow of a turning. Jonathan Harley had the good fortune to fall in with the companionship of Hermoine Kiddle, a lady of small stature but immense common sense, with Sam and Meggie Barldrop, and with Juliet. The lamps are lowered; the tinkling music of the piano starts; prompt is in his corner and the curtain is about to go up. Come with Alice Dwyer-Jones to recapture that almost lost, enchanting moment.

Alice Dwyer-Joyce

The Strolling Players

NEW YORK
ST. MARTIN'S PRESS

LONDON
ROBERT HALE & COMPANY

St. Martin's Press, Inc.
175 Fifth Avenue
New York, N.Y. 10010

Library of Congress Catalog Card Number 74-18735

Robert Hale & Company
63 Old Brompton Road
London S.W.7

ISBN 0 7091 4351 6

To Geraldine and Jack Myles,
of Birr, Ireland, I dedicate this
book.

Printed in Great Britain
Clarke, Doble & Brendon Ltd.,
Plymouth

THE STROLLING PLAYERS

I TOOK Sally Druce to an after-theatre supper at one of those small exclusive places, where the tables are set in dark alcoves, fit for any sort of romantic intrigue. I would have been far happier to have gone home and tumbled into my bed for a good night's sleep, for I was very tired indeed. I was in the strange grey no-man's-land of the mind, that was so familiar to me . . . still half the tragic Prince, I had just portrayed upon the stage, yet Jonathan Harley too, the renowned young actor, with the whole world at my feet.

There was a gypsy band roaming from table to table. It consisted of a girl with a piano-accordian, another with a jingling tambourine, and a swarthy individual with long side-whiskers and a fiddle tucked under his chin.

The girl with the tambourine looked as brown as old mahogany in the dim light, as indeed they all did. She had a head-dress of brightly coloured silk, with gold coins at her forehead, that flashed and tinkled at every move she made. Her ear-rings dangled to her shoulders and her eyes were as black as sloes. She sat down beside me and her face split into a brilliant melon-seed smile, as she asked me in a wheedling voice if I would like her to cast my horoscope.

Of course, Sally was delighted. She clapped her hands and laughed and said that she would hear the truth at last, and was as girlish as the Ophelia, she had just played on-stage.

The sloe eyes held misery in their depths. The smile went no further than her lips. She glanced momentarily at the swarthy man and he frowned at her. I thought it likely that there would be trouble later on, if she failed to make money from me, so I looked at her very gravely.

"I shall put you to the test," I pronounced. "Tell me under what sign of the Zodiac I was born, and the job is yours."

That should be easy enough for her. They must have known that a table was booked for me, and the man would have looked up my birthday in Who's Who, if he was as astute as he appeared to be. The girl looked at me keenly for a moment or so and I gave her a smile of encouragement. Her voice was very soft and low.

"You're an arrogant Leo," she said. "Your birthday must fall between the 24th July and the 24th August. It's clearly written for those that have the knowledge to read it . . . in the way you hold your head . . . in your wide forehead . . . in the tenderness of your mouth."

I laughed at her.

"You've got my birthday right at any rate. What else can you see?"

She looked down at the table as she went on. "You've been born with great gifts and the luck has come good for you to use them, so the sun shines on you and you have wealth and your name on the lips of many."

Of course, she must know who I was. It was all just a bit obvious.

"Yet, you're easily hurt for you hate lies and ugliness. Always . . . always, you seek for perfection and beauty."

Sally giggled a little.

"Can't you see any bad things?" she demanded and the girl turned her head with a jingling of the gold coins, to look at her.

"Your friend has a hot temper," she said in a serious voice. "And he seeks too much for praise. He wants to be the master and it is not good, that."

"Ha! Ha!" cried Sally in a melodramatic whisper. "Here come the guilty secrets."

The girl did not pay any more attention to her. She took my hand in hers and gazed earnestly into my eyes.

"Always . . . always . . . always, pride is your enemy. Learn to humble yourself, or you will never find the thing you seek. Kneel at the feet of your lady and you will find your dreams come true."

She turned my hand over and looked at the palm closely, and became all gypsy in a flash.

"Now I see into the future for you and tell you what is to come . . . if you cross my palm with silver."

It was the usual old stuff. I did not listen to half of it. After a while, I looked at my watch covertly, trying to repress the rudeness of a yawn.

"You're going to get a letter . . . a card perhaps . . . a piece of writing, in the space of one . . . one day, one month, one year. It will be nothing at the time, but it is a thing of great importance, for your happiness will depend on it . . . . "

I put my free hand into my pocket and took out my wallet. I had had enough of this. I gave her a pound and she thanked me and stood up with a little bobbing curtsey.

"I am telling you what is to come," she said with a strange insistence. "This letter . . . there are tears and sadness all about it. It's your passport to the dark lady, who will be your true love. Don't lose your way to her side, for she is waiting for you, till you come to her."

The swarthy man took the money out of her hand as neatly as a gull catching a piece of flung bread in one swoop. He tucked the fiddle under his chin and bowed to me and there was a gleam of gold in the whiteness of his teeth.

"Now we play specially for the great maestro. We play the true Romany music, for my mistress's heart here is broken. She is the fairest of all the women in the world, yet my little one says that it is a dark lady, who the maestro awaits. I think she not tell the fortune so good. Yes?"

Sally was bored with it all suddenly. She waved at the man to go away and leaned across the table to speak to me.

"I never heard such rubbish."

She did not care that the gypsy troupe heard her.

"It's just barefaced robbery . . . a way of begging without holding out the hat."

The gypsy girl had drawn back and was standing uncertainly at my side, looking down at me with her dark eyes drowned in wretchedness. I stood up and made a formal little bow.

"It was a very excellent fortune." I smiled. "I will endeavour to curb my pride and my temper and all the doubtful things you mentioned. I will watch the post every day for this letter and when it comes, I will lock it up in the Bank of England, and I thank you for all the trouble you've taken with me tonight."

Yet I was telling her a pack of lies, for I went on living in the way I had always lived. I did not watch the post every day either for that matter. Worst of all, when the piece of writing came, I was fool enough not to place any importance upon it, and I certainly never thought of locking it up in the Bank of England.

I swung my legs out of bed the next morning, stretched my arms towards the ceiling and yawned. Westlake picked up my dressing gown and held it out for me and I shrugged my shoulders into it and tightened the sash around my waist. I yawned again at my reflection in the mirror over the basin a minute later and ran my hand over my chin.

"It shouldn't take me too long to grow that beard . . . a month or six weeks perhaps. I want to get a neat line of hair along the angle of the jaw . . . Spanish style, I suppose."

My secretary was watching me in the glass.

"I think it will be most becoming, J.H. The ladies will write and implore you not to shave it off again, when you come out of show."

"Blast the ladies!" I said shortly. "God! That affair last night was boring and I was dog tired. There were too many people talking too loudly in too small a space and not enough air for a cat to breathe. Then I had three hours of unadulterated Sally Druce in such a dim light that one couldn't see what one was eating. There should be a Society for the Prevention of Cruelty to Actors, you know."

He grinned at me.

"A Society to prevent people from killing the cat by feeding him too much cream?" he suggested.

"One gets so sick of being fawned upon," I grumbled. "I often wish that some honest body would come into my dressing-room and say "you were bloody bad, tonight, Jonathan Harley. I never heard Bill Shakespeare so bastard-ised before, and for God's sake, stop talking as if you have a sore throat, when you're pretending to be emotional. Why don't you suck a cough drop?""

I finished shaving in silence and put the razor down peevishly.

"Oh God!" I yawned, "I'm still half asleep and my head aches."

I strewed the dressing gown and the top of my pyjamas on the floor, as I made for the shower and heard Westlake sigh as he retrieved them for me. He followed me into the bathroom and threw me the bath-sheet, as I gasped out from under the icy hail of water two minutes later.

I went into breakfast and stared moodily at the glass of orange juice, while Westlake prepared to go through the correspondence with me. He put an elegant envelope by my plate and raised a brow at me.

"This is marked 'Private and Confidential' ", he told me and went off to perch on the edge of the desk to watch me open it.

I transferred my frown from the orange juice to the letter and sighed with irritation, because I saw it was from Sally Druce.

"Ophelia again! What in the name of perdition can she find to write to me about this morning? Merciful heaven! She was with me till two o'clock."

Westlake retired to his chair behind the desk and put

the letters in a neat pile. I could see that he was thinking "So he calls her 'Ophelia' off stage now."

I opened the letter with a grunt and read it quickly and he smiled when I threw it down on top of an open dish of marmalade, for he disliked Miss Druce.

"What do you think of her?" I asked him. "Come now. Let's have an honest opinion."

"What do I think of whom?" he asked, trying to hedge.

"My private and confidential lady friend."

He looked at me primly.

"I suppose it was from Miss Druce?" he said. "Of course, I didn't open it, as it was marked 'Private.'"

"You won't get out of it as easily as all that. You're the only honest man about me. Let's have a candid opinion of Ophelia and I do not ask it in any mood of frivolity."

He glanced down at the first letter on the pile on the desk.

"We really should be getting through these. It's gone twelve and you've got a luncheon appointment in Soho at half past one. You're not even dressed."

"What do you think of her?" I pursued.

"Miss Druce is a very good actress. You know that. You picked her straight out of R.A.D.A. and made her a star. Your judgement is never wrong in these things."

"And as a woman?" I demanded.

He looked at me doggedly.

"She's very pretty. She's good company. She's gay and witty."

I put on my horn-rimmed glasses and looked down at the thick deckle-edged note-paper.

"Darling, darling, darling Johnnie . . . " I read to myself and raised my brows at him.

"And?"

"She's very fond of you. Of course, she's good reason to be, for you've put her where she stands today. That's obvious."

I took my glasses off and threw them onto the table with a clatter.

"Did you say she was obvious?" I asked.

He was flustered for once.

"Good Lord, no, J.H. I only said it was obvious that she should be grateful to you."

"Pity!" I sighed. "It's not like you to evade a question. I thought you were being candid for once."

"We really should be getting on with the business of the day," he reminded me.

I tore the letter into fragments and scattered them like confetti on the table. Then I spread marmalade on a finger of toast and ate it. I sat sipping my coffee and there was a silence in the room, except for the undertone of Park Lane's traffic from far below.

"Very well then," I said at last. "You are disinclined to discuss my private life, so I'll write your lines for you, though I can't see why you should object to telling me to my face what you think of the infernal Druce. She's pretty and witty and gay. She'll go far in her chosen profession. She's a good leading lady. She'd probably make a charming mistress . . . certainly a willing one. She's obvious. She's persistent and she's damned tenacious."

"She's very much in love with you," he put in quietly.

"Love! Bah!"

I picked a cigarette out of the silver box and he came across the room to light it for me.

"The girl doesn't know what love is," I snorted. "I've

yet to meet a girl who does and I don't think I ever will.
Great God above! Why am I damned to be the object of
infatuation of every silly girl, who pays a few pieces of
silver to see me act? I'm sick of women, who look at me
sideways out of their stupid calf's eyes, and now even
you can't give me an honest opinion."

He picked up some letters from the desk.

"There are a number of requests here for your autographed picture," he said drily. "All from young ladies."

"Blast my autographed picture!"

"There's an invitation for you to go up to Cranston, as
guest of honour for Speech Day," he went on.

"Refuse it."

"But it's your old school, J.H." he protested, but I
ignored him and asked what else there was to be seen to.

"There's a casket of cigarettes from a tobacco company.
They would like your opinion on the cigarette. It's a
luxury one. It has extra length and a filter tip. They would
be very honoured if they could market it under your
name and you would get the usual . . . . "

"No," I cried angrily.

He looked across at me.

"It's a very generous offer," he pointed out.

"Tell them what they can do with it."

I stood up and threw the cigarette I was smoking into
the fireplace and he looked at me, as if I were a wayward
child.

"There are twenty invitations of one sort or another,
all due for your holiday period. I presume I write and
decline with thanks?"

"Your presumption is correct."

"You really should begin to dress, you know. There are

a few people waiting to see you."

He gave me their cards and I glanced at them with a sigh.

"These have all been sent over from Actors Anonymous, as you call them," I said. "Go and sort them out. My head aches. I'll not see anybody. They just want money and you can deal with that. They'll be less embarrassed with you. And get Sally Druce on the phone. Ask her to come here to pick me up. Tell her I'm delayed and see if she'll pick Salvage up on the way and come on here for drinks."

He went off and I sat on the desk and glanced through the notices in the papers. They had let me off lightly as usual. One even said that I had restored Shakespeare to the living theatre, whatever he meant by that.

It was fifteen minutes before Westlake came back and by that time, I was half asleep in an armchair. He had a card in his hand.

"I've got rid of them, all except one," he told me. "They were deserving cases and I gave out the usual largesse and said that you'd look out for any vacancies you could think of."

"Whom must I place now?" I asked him drily.

"Ann Perry would be grateful for anything. She won't part with that child you know and Peter can't help her. He's got a wife already and he says that the child wasn't his, which we all know it was. She hasn't a chance with a child trotting at her heels, but she's determined not to let her go to a home. She had the little girl outside. Belinda's her name and she's a lovely child. Ann's got a job as a housekeeper, but she wants to stage a come-back . . . . "

I thought of Ann Perry playing Eliza Doolittle, when I was starting what they called my meteoric career.

"Ann Perry," I reflected. "She was a fool. There's not a

chance in a million that she'll ever act again. She'd better stick to her domestic post. Good housekeepers are scarce and she might marry her employer."

"I said that you'd think about it, J.H."

I looked at him irritably.

"I'll think about it, all right. I'm thinking about it now and what a fool she made of herself about that ass. Who else was there?"

"Old Hollidge was there too. You know that he's got arthritis. He can't hold down a job . . . not one like he's had."

"Bert Hollidge?" I exclaimed. "The stage manager? Good God! He writes too. He'll have to fall back on that."

"He's got arthritis in his wrists. He can't hold a pen."

"Poor Hollidge! A tape recorder would be the thing for him to get. Of course, his stage managing career is over for all time, poor devil."

I looked at Westlake enquiringly.

"And who was the persistent one?" I asked him. "Whom must I interview personally, when the great Bert Hollidge has been turned from my door?"

"She's a very pretty girl."

I got up and walked across the room to the mantlepiece.

"I'm sick of pretty persistent girls," I cried and turned round to face him wrathfully. "What the hell does she want and it's no good telling me, because I won't see her."

"She's representing Joshua Mardall's Company of Strolling Players. She wants to know if you would do them the great honour of going out to the coast, when you go up to Edinburgh for the Festival. She'd like you to give a personal appearance at their show. She's a nice girl and she's obviously keyed up to beard the lion in his den.

She's very shy and reticent . . . not far from tears too, I imagine."

"God defend me from shy reticent weeping maidens!" I burst out, and Westlake frowned a little in disaproval, as he always did at such demonstrations on my part.

"She saw that speech of yours in the press," he explained primly. "She came to ask for help."

I thrust my two hands deep into the pockets of my dressing gown and glared at him.

"Is my cheque not good enough for her?" I demanded. "Does she think it'll bounce?"

"I think you ought to see her," he said quietly. "She's not the usual run of girl. This Joshua Mardall's her Grandfather and he brought her up since her parents died. She feels she owes him everything and the show's about on the rocks."

I turned my back on him and frowned at myself in the mirror over the mantlepiece.

"So I'm to travel up to this place, where-ever it is, and make a personal appearance on the stage, with her cheap little company, so that she can pay off her debts?"

My voice was high with exasperation.

"Is the girl mad? Who are these people? Joshua Mardall's Company of Players? Great God almighty! I never heard of them. It's probably some twelfth rate company, playing the seaside resorts in the season. And Scotland too! No! No! No! No! Give her a cheque and tell her to clear out and if she doesn't go, take her by the back of the neck and throw her down the stairs."

I looked at my watch.

"Is Sally calling for me?"

He turned back from the door.

"She says that she'll pick up Mr. Salvage and bring him along as you said."

"Very well. For heaven's sake, get rid of that girl before they arrive and see to the drinks."

He went off registering disapproval of me in the trim of his shoulders, but he was back in ten seconds.

"She's gone," he said. "The door was ajar. She must have heard every word you said."

He gave me a cardbroad ticket.

"She left that on the arm of her chair. It's a ticket for a show of some sort at a place called Lismore next month."

I read the words pencilled across the face of it.

"I see, sir, you are liberal in offers.
You taught me how to beg and now, methinks,
You teach me how a beggar should be answered . . . . "

I held it out to Westlake.

"Did you see this?" I cried. "She must have written it. By God! She quotes Portia too."

His mouth drawstringed in.

"I think you should have seen her."

"That's quite obvious!" I retorted in a rage. "You think I should see all these beggars who pluck at my skirts. Don't you understand that it's your job to act as a barrier between them and me. Merciful heavens! I sign the cheques for you. You only have to do a tactful hand-out. They like it better that way."

He had gone to look out through the window.

"There she is now," he remarked. "I think she's crying."

"Why must I always be surrounded with hysterical women?" I demanded irritably, and went over to look down at her. I could only see the defeated set of her thin shoulders, under her navy gaberdine coat, and the top of her dark head. She turned up the collar of the coat, as if she felt the cold and dabbed quickly at her eyes with a handkerchief, and I felt the miserable feeling I always get in my chest, when I see a woman crying.

"Oh, to hell and blazes with it!" I said and watched her go across the road. "Get in touch with her and buy some tickets for her wretched show or make some kind of gesture."

He took the ticket from my hand and shook his head.

"There's no address, but I suppose we might get in touch with them, when they play at Lismore. They're not listed anywhere as a company of actors. They must be a small group . . . perhaps amateurs. Lismore is away up in the Highlands of Scotland . . . miles from anywhere."

I watched her disappear from view.

"She knows her Shakespeare," I observed, feeling that I had behaved very badly and wishing that the whole incident could be undone.

"She's not much more than a school-girl," he said and I tried to ease my feelings of sarcasm, as is my base custom.

"I suppose she played 'Portia' in Students' night," I remarked drily and he looked at me more disapprovingly than ever, so that I tightened the sash of my dressing gown and went off to dress, feeling thoroughly put out.

"What did she expect me to do?" I demanded before I shut the door with a slam. "Act Bassanio opposite her in the 'Merchant'. Does she know who I am?"

I was standing at the dressing table ten minutes later in my trousers and shirt, knotting my tie, when Ophelia burst in upon me, with Westlake hard on her heels.

"You can't go in there, Miss Druce," he was protesting. "Mr. Harley is dressing."

She flung her bag across the room on to my bed and came over to stand behind me, putting her arm in its mink muff about my neck.

"Of course, I can, Westlake," she pouted back across her shoulder at him. "Johnnie doesn't mind me coming in, when he's dressing, do you darling?"

She kissed my cheek and the sophisticated fresh-pared pencil smell of her scent smoked up into my nostrils, as she turned me round and smiled at me.

"I'll do your tie, Johnnie," she said and she took a long time about it too, with much grimacing of her pretty face and pursing-up of her dark orange mouth.

Westlake looked at me helplessly and wondered if it would be more tactful of him to leave us alone, but I shook my head at him slightly, and at last he came across the room to pick up my jacket and hold it out for me.

"Salvage is a pig," Miss Druce was saying. "He says that he doesn't see me as Mary. He wants a dark girl . . . somebody he knows in Dublin, with a stupid name. He says that my face is all wrong."

"Your face is all right," I smiled. "He's all wrong there."

"Don't joke about it, darling," she said. "I don't like Salvage and I don't like his play."

I looked at the curves of her pencilled brows, and put up a hand to feel the softness of her blond hair.

"Mary, Queen of Scots was beautiful," I said. "I see her as very dark, with a creamy skin and lovely dark blue eyes, with her hair black in a 'V' on her white forehead . . . tall and slender and regal."

"She was in your hall this morning then." Westlake put in suddenly. "And you turned her away."

"Ann Perry?" I said. "She's not dark."

"The other girl . . . the one from the Strolling Players."

"Ah, Portia," I mused, and Sally took me by the shoulders and gave me a shake.

"I can have a black rinse," she argued. "Am I not regal enough for you? I want to play Mary."

She was behaving ridiculously like a small girl, who wanted something she could not have.

"You're in love with her already," she challenged me. "You're always in love with your leading ladies. Everybody knows that."

I put an arm round her and guided her towards the door to the sitting room.

"In a few months from now, I'll be James Hepburn, Earl of Bothwell, my dearest one," I explained. "Her Majesty, the Queen of Scotland will be tiring of her consort, Darnley. She'll recall the Earl of Bothwell to her side, and she'll fall in love with him. Of course, he'll be in love with her. He must be to make it come out the way he does, when the curtain goes up, and they all come back to life, but there's no reality in it, any more than there is to a dream."

I left her sitting beside Salvage, the play-wright, and went to pour their drinks, but when I sat down, she came to perch herself on the arm of my chair and put her hand up to tickle the back of my neck.

"Do you realize what schizophrenics you make of us?" I asked Salvage. "When you write such stuff, they all come out of history and live again . . . Mary and Darnley and Bothwell and poor little Riccio, who cowers against her skirts again, when they come to do him to death."

I stood up and went to the fireplace to get away from Ophelia's attentions, but she followed me and put her arm about my waist and held up the mink muff to my face in an absurd way to pretend it was my new beard.

She was pretty and gay and childish. She had made a wonderful Ophelia, but she would never do for the regal Queen of Scotland . . . the ardent, beautiful, regal Queen of Scotland. Salvage was right about that.

"Do you like the play?" he asked me eagerly and I tried to ignore Ophelia's kittenish behaviour. I looked over at Salvage and wondered how such a middle-aged bald old man could get such magic to come out of his pen onto paper. He had thick pebbled glasses and a paunch, which hung down between his legs.

"I told you," I said. "You re-create them and larger than life too, I suppose. They could never have lived or moved or spoken with such perfection. It can't miss. You'll see. They'll love it."

"And I can play Mary?" insisted my Ophelia.

I turned her round and shoved her across the room towards Salvage.

"Go and flirt with the author then, for he'll have a say in it, and it seems that he disapproves of blondes."

He got as red as a coal, as she went over and sat on the arm of his chair and leaned against his shoulder. She was hoping that I was jealous of old Salvage, and I regretted for a moment that I had not seen the girl from Joshua Mardall's Strolling Players. She cropped up into my mind for no reason at all. I had said to Westlake that I wanted to meet a girl, who knew what love was and I found myself wondering if she would have been capable of it. She was certainly not infatuated with me and she was not out for money. She had been independent enough, and proud enough too, to leave. She had been scornful enough to write the chiding message across the face of the ticket.

"I see, sir, you are liberal in offers . . . . "

Westlake had said that she had seen some speech of mine, but I could not recall having made any offers in a recent speech. I put her out of my mind and turned my attention back to my guests.

"I have seen Mr. Harley coming off stage between scenes," Westlake was saying. "And he's no more Jonathan Harley than he's The Emperor of China. He's Hamlet or Othello or Lear. Then he shakes his head and pulls himself together and he's his own man again."

Ophelia was back with her arm about my shoulders.

"I must remember that when we go up to Edinburgh next week for the Festival run of Hamlet. I must catch him on stage. Is that how it's done, Westlake?"

He looked very embarrassed and I stood up and suggested that we make a move to the Restaurant. It was the same old procedure that I was so used to by now . . . the sudden recognition, the pointed finger, the whispered word.

"Isn't that Jonathan Harley? And surely that's the girl, who played Ophelia last night?"

"Could I have your autograph, Mister?"

"Excuse me, sir, but the lady at the corner table would like you to accept a bottle of Champagne with her compliments and congratulations."

"Could you be so kind as to autograph this photograph of yourself for me? I admire your work so much."

"Hello, old boy! I haven't seen you lately. What's all this we hear about a great new play? James Hepburn, Earl of Bothwell? Who was he, when he was at home? Scottish historical? Good God! What next?"

Salvage was new enough to the game to enjoy the lime of publicity, but I was sick and tired of it.

"Blast it!" I exclaimed. "I'd like to go away and live on a desert island for a year and see nobody at all. I'm sick of the human race."

Ophelia's muff came coaxingly under my chin, and I restrained myself from taking it from her arm and throwing it at a fat woman two tables away, who chewed her food like a cow chewing its cud, and never took her eyes from my face.

"Why don't you borrow my cottage in the Highlands, Johnnie? You could have it for as long as you liked and it's a hundred miles from anywhere. The nearest big town is Oban and that's a small place, and anyway, it's miles and miles away. You could grow your blessed beard and learn your part and not see a soul from one week's end to the next."

"I wonder, saire, if there would be any possibility of getting two seats for the opening night of your new show, Bosswell? They say it will all be sold out and people will put advertisements in the papers to try and get places, but my wife, she is one of your most greatest fans, saire . . . . "

I looked at the waiter with fury and the head waiter bore down on our table.

"Was something wrong, Mr. Harley?" he bowed, as if I were a blasted idol and I opened my mouth to tell him what I thought of his waiter, but Ophelia was flickering her false eyelashes at him.

"Everything's fine, Stephano. We were just saying how marvellous this prawn thing is. Will you compliment the Chef and tell him that Mr. Harley likes it very much? We must have it, when we come in again."

I looked at her with distaste and wondered how I could come so near to loving her on stage, with her pathetic "garlands of long purples" and her "rosemary for remembrance." She had no birth nor breeding nor beauty of spirit and every move she made was obvious. She was trying to get me into a corner, from which I should have no escape, but to climb into her bed and that I was very loath to do.

"It's really a Highland croft, darling."

I came back to the crowded restaurant and heard Ophelia's voice above the parrot-house chatter. "There are no amenities . . . just none, but it doesn't seem to matter. It's a grey stone cottage, with two rooms. There's no gas or electricity . . . primitive really. No mod. cons. and you cook with oil and you have candles for lighting."

I smiled at her.

"So you go to bed by candlelight?"

"Stop flirting with me and listen," she laughed. "There's no water except the sea, and there's a little river, that comes down the hill at the side of the house, with the cutest waterfall. You've got to boil the drinking water. The place is high up in the sky on the top of a tremendous cliff. You've got to shut the gate, or cars come in at night and crash over."

"It sounds idyllic," I said with sarcasm, frowning at a girl across the room, who was trying to get up the courage to come over and ask us for our autographs.

"Don't be tiresome. Cars don't crash over. You make sure you keep the gate closed. The lane to the croft goes straight on and the road itself turns round and if the gate isn't shut, you think the lane's the road and it goes over the cliff."

I looked at her gravely.

"If I accept your very kind offer, I will keep the gate closed," I promised. "I object to the noise of cars crashing over cliffs at night."

"And will you accept my offer?"

I wondered for a moment if she went with the cottage and rather fancied that she did.

"It's near a town called Lismore," she said and the name was vaguely familiar.

"Lismore," I murmured. "Lismore."

"It sounds like poetry the way you say it," she whispered in my ear and then Westlake gave me the clue.

"The ticket," he said. "You remember. The Strolling Players will be there next month. If you spend your holiday in Miss Druce's croft, you can tender your apologies in person."

"Apologies?" I shot out at him and he smiled deprecatingly.

"I'm sure that you will agree that apologies are due."

"To whom?" I asked him. "To Portia? To your Royal Mary, Queen of Scotland?"

He looked down at his plate.

"Indeed yes. That last title fitted her very well, and you said some pretty hurtful things."

There was no doubt in my mind that he was right.

The thought of the incident irked me with a strange insistency. I kept thinking of the way she had turned up the collar of her coat, although the day was warm. She had shrunk down inside it and I fancied she had done it to get away from the cruelty of my words.

"Who is this Mary, Queen of Scotland?" Sally asked petulantly, picking small potato straws from my plate with her fingers and eating them. "Is she somebody I should be jealous of?"

I told her not to be foolish and Salvage frowned at us through his pebbled glasses and said that he was really very sorry but that he would not be at all happy with Miss Druce in the part. He was finishing another play and there was a part in it that would be tailor-made for her. They talked about it and argued back and forth and then we were on the pavement outside the Restaurant, with people stopping to stare at us. We dropped her off at her flat and let Salvage out at his club and finally Westlake and I arrived home again. I had eaten and drunk far too much and my head was muzzy. I would have liked to go to bed, but there was endless work to be done, if I was to get up to Edinburgh on schedule. The daily woman came into the sitting room soon after we got back, with a newspaper in her hand and set it on the desk in front of me.

"Is this yours, sir?" she asked me. "I found it stuffed down under the back of the cushion in one of the hall chairs. Did you want it kept? It's got that big speech of yours, centre page, all turned out ready to read."

She tapped it with her finger and I saw the bold print heading.

APPEAL BY JONATHAN HARLEY

I remembered the whole affair in a flash and got the same feeling of misery in my breast, as when I had seen the girl crying. Westlake had written the blasted speech for me and like a fool, I had not given it much thought. It was pretty trite stuff and I shuddered as I remembered the quotation at the finish. It was the sort of thing you would see, written in ye olde worlde English on a tuppeny postcard.

"I EXPECT TO PASS THROUGH THIS WORLD BUT ONCE. ANY GOOD THING THEREFORE THAT I CAN DO, OR ANY KINDNESS THAT I CAN SHOW TO ANY FELLOW CREATURE, LET ME DO IT NOW' LET ME NOT DEFER IT OR NEGLECT IT, FOR I SHALL NOT PASS THIS WAY AGAIN."

"The girl had that paper in her hand." Westlake said. "That's why she came to you. I told you she'd read it, didn't I? You were appealing for the Fund and there was a tremendous response. The Secretary said it was practically entirely due to that speech."

I waved to the daily woman to go away and put my head in my hands.

"Your speech," I contradicted him. "You wrote it, blast you!"

"But you delivered it," he laughed. "I didn't even recognize it, the way you put it over. It's that sincere voice of yours, you know . . . the clarity and the silver, and then the slight huskiness of emotion."

I got to my feet and scowled at him.

"Sincerity!" I said through my gritted teeth. "Don't talk such rubbish and what's more, don't write it in future, if I ask you for a simple speech. Look what you've let me in for this time."

I threw the paper at him and he caught it and folded it neatly back into position like the old woman he was. He put it gently into the waste paper basket and looked mildly across the desk at me and I saw the hurt in his eyes.

"I'm sorry," I said shortly. "The fault's mine, not yours. It always is when I shout at you. I'm a confounded fool. Take no notice of me."

I went off towards the door of the bedroom, feeling

disgusted with myself and I turned to look back at him, with my hand on the door knob.

"I'll make a restitution somehow. I don't know how, but I'll think of something. It would be a just penance if I had to go up to Lismore and appear in her blasted show."

He looked startled, as well he might.

"You couldn't do that . . . " he started.

"Of course, I couldn't," I agreed. "I'll send them an anonymous donation. I'll think something out in a day or two. It was unforgivable of me to make the Queen of Scotland weep."

"Queen of Scotland!" he echoed.

"You called her that yourself," I reminded him. "I didn't even see the damned girl properly. That seems to be the cause of the whole trouble, doesn't it?"

I went up to Edinburgh by night the next week with the full company and we got quite a reception at Prince's Street Station. There were the usual reporters and press photographers, and there was even a unit from the B.B.C. television studios, who wanted shots of us for some programme they were doing for the Festival. I stood with my arm round Ophelia's shoulders, as we were interviewed against the background of the echoing station.

We had breakfast in my suite at the hotel and went straight to the theatre afterwards for a run through of the play. It was one of those days, when everything goes wrong. Polonius had laryngitis and could scarcely make himself heard beyond the first row of the stalls, but he would not let his understudy take over and said that he would be quite all right by the evening, which was clearly impossible. The props were never in their places at the right time and the electricians ran into some major trouble with some special lighting we wanted, and we had a blackout for half an hour, which did nothing to improve our tempers.

I have a name for being easy to work with, but I was impossible that day. I quarrelled with the chief electrician, the stage manager, the producer, and most of the principles.

"We'll never get the blasted show on tonight," I said at last in the grave-digging scene. I threw poor Yorick's skull at Horatio and Ophelia appeared from the wings, still in costume and draped a garland of her wild flowers around my brow.

"To be or not to be, that is the question," she giggled and everybody laughed. I turned on my heel and went out into the stalls to sulk by myself. Ophelia followed me repentantly and sat in the seat behind me to twine both her arms round my neck.

"You taught me how to make jokes and now you're cross with me, when I make them."

"God!" I thought. "Here's another of them. "You taught me how to beg . . . . And now methinks you teach me how a beggar should be answered."

"I'm sorry," I muttered ungraciously. "You know how I am on these occasions. We've got to get it running smoothly. We'll have a pretty discriminating audience out front tonight and it's got to be perfect."

She rubbed her face against the back of my neck like a

little kitten.

"It will be perfect," she sighed. "It always is. You'll be a bundle of bad temper and nerves and then you'll be on and you won't put a foot wrong. You never do."

They all knew how I suffered before I went on.

Bill, my dresser, looked at me sympathetically that night, as I sat in front of the glaring lights and began to make up for the show.

"This is always the worst part for you, sir. It'll soon be over."

I looked at my reflection in the mirror and saw how the wrinkles were coming at the sides of my eyes and along my forehead. I could not remember one line of my part. "To be or not to be, that is the question," I thought suddenly, but it would be a poor showing if I could think of no more of it. My hands were shaking and I took deep breaths and tried to pull myself together. I cursed myself for the thousandth time for getting mixed up with such a career.

"Ten minutes, Mr. Harley."

It seemed a long, long time before I stood in the wings with the others and waited for the curtain to go up on Act One, Scene Two . . . a room of state in the Castle. I fidgeted nervously with the sash of my doublet and the King smiled at me.

"I wish I had your waistline, Hamlet."

The houselights would be going down now and the curtain would slide up. Yes, there it was and the King went into his opening speech, as the Court moved on stage. I let them get settled in their places and then I went on and the applause crackled across the lights like machine gun fire. It went on far longer than it would have done in town. I bent down to kiss the Queen's hand.

"You'll slow the show up, Hamlet," she murmured. "They adore you in Edinburgh."

Of course, the applause was not all for me, I thought, as I moved round to stand behind her chair. What use would I be without Bill Shakespeare's immortal words in my mouth? If I could remember any of my lines, that was, I amended to myself wryly.

"It seems, sir, you are generous in offers,
    You taught me how to beg . . . . "

That was what the girl had written across the ticket, but it was from the Merchant of Venice.

I heard the King's voice and my cue: "And now my cousin Hamlet, and my son . . . . "

I heard the familiar words spoken by my own voice and the panic dropped from me like a cloak: "A little more than kin and less than kind."

We had some of the asides recorded and this was one of them. I did not speak, but my voice was heard, to represent my thoughts. We had found it very effective, but it took some smart timing off stage.

"How is it that the clouds still hang on you?" the King asked me and I answered "Not so, my lord, I am too much i' the sun. . . ."

I was not Jonathan Harley any more. The miracle had come about for me as it always did. I was the tragic Prince of Denmark, brooding on my father's death with the world all "weary, stale, flat and unprofitable."

The play ran its course smoothly and at last it was all over. We took curtain after curtain, and I thought that they would never let us go. I stood with Ophelia's hand in mine and made a speech, which Westlake had written for me. As I bowed, I thought of his words in the flat. "It's that sincere voice of yours, you know, the clarity and the silver and then the slight huskiness . . . . "

I kissed Ophelia's hand.

"I'll take that cottage," I murmured and smiled at her.

"I'm so glad, darling. It's an enchanted place . . . . "

On the last night of the run, we went on to supper in some over-noisy, over-crowded place. I seemed to be surrounded with chattering women for hour after hour. They gushed flattery and adulation over me and linked their arms in mine. They grasped both my hands or kissed my cheek, till I was nauseated with the Vanity Fair, that swirled round me.

At one stage, Ophelia came across and slipped her arm through mine and I smelt the scented gin from her breath.

"You're making a smash hit with your lady fans tonight, Johnnie," she smiled. "Are you trying to make me jealous, for if you are, you're succeeding?"

"Stop talking nonsense," I told her. "The only thing that's stopping me going home to my bed this instant, is the thought that I'm off to your cottage in the morning. Don't forget to let me have the key sometime."

She was a little drunk. She waved her glass at me and the drink slopped over onto the carpet.

"You don't have to have a key," she smiled. "You go to Lismore and you call at Mrs. Stewart's shop in the Main Street. She looks after the place, when I'm not there, which is nearly all the time. Fiona McLeod will be behind the counter. She's Mrs. Stewart's niece. If Mrs. Stewart's out, Fiona will give you the key."

I took the glass out of her hand and put it on the table. "You've had enough to drink," I said, but she took no notice of me. She picked up my drink, which I had put down ten minutes before and drained it down in one gulp, and I thought of the hang-over she was going to have in the morning.

"Get on the telephone and ring me, when you get lonely. There's one in Mrs. Stewart's shop. I'll come up for the week end."

I smiled at her and wondered if she knew how distasteful I found her. People thought I was having an affair with her, and she did nothing to make them think otherwise, and neither did I for that matter. It was strange the way the miracle happened for me. On stage, she would be beautiful and desirable. Then the final curtain would come down and there would be the limbo of confusion between stage and dressing room, as the dream faded to reality. It was always the same. Only Westlake knew the purity of my intimate life. I sometimes wondered if he knew that I was weary of waiting for a dream to come true . . . waiting to find a woman, who would love me for myself alone and not for the trappings of fame and fortune.

"Promise," said Ophelia at my side.

"Promise what?"

"You weren't even listening to me," she scolded. "Promise you'll ring me when you get lonely."

"I promise," I said and felt tired of her bright smile and her sleek hair and her orange red lips. Yet on stage, she was all innocence and youth . . . all softness and kittenishness and purity, like a maiden, not long left school. That was what Westlake had said about the girl from the Strolling Players. I frowned and refused to think of the impression I must have made upon her. I might look her up, when they came to Lismore and pass it off some way . . . say I was tired and that I had not seen how pretty she was . . . make a joke of it and flirt with her a little . . . buy a row of stalls in whatever theatre they played and send her in an enormous extravagant armful of flowers.

I got back to the hotel in the small hours of the morning and found that they had a fire blazing up the chimney and ice for the drinks in a thermos flask. I took off my jacket and put on a dressing gown and a soft cravat and then I sat down with a sigh in one of the deep armchairs and stretched out my legs before me.

"And now for a few weeks of peace," I said to Westlake. "When you see me again, I'll be a Scots nobleman, with a bearded face and a Highland lilt to my tongue. Then we'll go into rehearsal and start the same old treadmill all over again."

"It's the price of fame," he reminded me, and put a tumbler of Old Mull into my hand.

He filled a drink out for himself and turned off all the lights, except the reading lamp on the table behind my head.

"Is it worth it?" I asked him and listened to the ice clinking against the side of the glass. He glanced across at me and then went to sit down in the chair on the other side of the fire.

"Indeed it is," he assured me earnestly. "You bring pleasure to millions. You've put a new interpretation to plays, that the mass of people considered as dry as dust.

You're a kind of National monument, I suppose . . . a man England can be proud of. They say that you'll get a knighthood in the next honours list."

"A knighthood!" I said scornfully. "To my mind, a knighthood is reserved for the pure gentlemen in armour, who perform deeds of valour and bravery. There's nothing of the knight about me and never has been."

He got up and stood with his back half turned to me, so that his face was in shadow, as he gazed down at the fire.

"That's where you're wrong. You always underrate yourself. You've worked like a slave to get to the position you hold today. You never spare yourself. You'd not rest now, if your doctor hadn't ordered it. You've walked the tight-rope to fame and you've avoided falling into the mire. You could have been a very different sort of chap, but you've held onto your ideals, haven't you?"

"Don't talk rubbish," I laughed. "I thought that you knew me better than anybody else, but now I see that you're just another fan."

He took no notice of me. He might well have been talking to himself.

"I owe you a lot one way or another. We've been friends for a very long time. When Sheila died, I was finished, but you gave me something to fill in the time . . . . "

It was not like him to talk about Sheila. I wondered what had made him do it tonight. Perhaps he had felt as lonely as I had done, in that crowded room.

"You were lucky to have had Sheila for a wife," I said quietly. "You don't often find people like her."

He turned round to look down at me.

"I have to get this off my chest," he sighed. "Shout at

me if you like, when I'm finished, but hear me out first."

I nodded my head.

"All these beautiful ladies of yours . . . " he began and paused before he went on. "I've seen so many of them come and so many of them go. They're not the ones for you. Don't get mixed up with Sally Druce. I know it's an impertinence of me to say this, but I am a very old friend and you tell me that I'm candid and honest. You've given an impression that you're very struck on her and this cottage business might be tricky. She's not the one, you're waiting for."

I sat and put my drink down on the table by my hand.

"And how do you know I'm waiting for any woman?" I demanded, my voice high with irritation.

"She'll come," he said in the same quiet way. "One day, you'll find her. Don't get entangled with these creatures of tinsel. They're not real. Their attraction is illusion. They go down with the house-lights, when the show is over and the people are gone home and the floor is littered with empty chocolate wrappings and cigarette ends."

I stood up and yawned. Then I went over and laid a hand on his shoulder and tried to ease the tension by laughter.

"If Ophelia comes anywhere near the infernal cottage, I'll run for my life," I said. "I wanted a place to hole up in from humanity and Lismore is as good as any. Besides, I have to make my peace with the Queen of Scotland, as you commanded."

I went off towards the hall.

"Don't worry. If I could wed Ophelia on stage and live out my life under the lights, it might be a different matter, but she's not for me. I promise you. My God, Westlake!

Loyalty is demanded in marriage. You've heard Sally Druce talking about her friends behind their backs. Don't you think that I realise what her acid little tongue says about me, when I'm not there? Oh, no, old chap. You'll drive me out to the coast tomorrow . . . it's today now, I suppose. You can go away and forget me for a few weeks. I'll come to no harm. I'll get involved with nobody but James Hepburn, Earl of Bothwell."

I got into bed and thought of the woman I was waiting for. I saw myself at her feet, pleading for her love. I imagined how I would bury my face against her dress and how her hand would come down to stroke the back of my head. I imagined how I would take her into my arms, her dark eyes all luminous and tender and then I slept like a log, and did not wake till the waiter came to tell me that breakfast was laid on the table in the sitting-room.

We left Edinburgh shortly after lunch and ran quickly up across Scotland. After Callender, the country was more beautiful with every mile we passed. The traffic was heavy and the road was winding. I was tired by the time we got to the sea, and neither of us was sorry, to see the first grey stone houses of Lismore. We drove into the Main Street and stopped outside the General Stores. I got out to stretch my legs and walked along the straggling street by the sea front, that was all there was of the town. Westlake had gone to arrange matters with Mrs. Stewart, get the key and find out where the cottage was. He came after me in two minutes.

"It's no good," he told me. "Mrs. Stewart is gone to hospital in Oban for an operation and there's nobody else to look after you. The local girls all work at the hotel down the coast. It seems that there's a labour shortage even here."

"So now, what do we do?"

"I got the key," he told me. "I thought that you'd like to look at the place. We might even camp out there for the night and find somewhere else in the morning. The hotel might be passable."

We climbed back into the car and set off along the coast road to the north. It deteriorated after the first mile and soon it was just two tracks for the wheels, with grass growing tall between them. The surface deteriorated too. We bumped and jolted along in a most uncomfortable manner, with the sea below us on the right.

"It's a white gate on the coast side of the road," Westlake said. "The name's painted on it. It's called 'Tir-nan-oge.' They said it was not far out . . . about two miles, and we can't miss it."

It felt more like five we both agreed, before the road seemed to come to a halt at a white painted gate. Then I saw that it did not really end, but turned very sharply round to the left, to run inland.

"That's Ophelia's gate," I laughed, as I got out to open it. "You know the one, we must never leave open. It's not surprising."

I closed it with the same difficulty as I had opened it and we went along a grassy lane for a hundred yards and then we swung abruptly through a grove of hazel trees to come out onto a plateau of short tough blue-green sea grass. The cottage was fifty yards back from the cliff edge and it was the usual crofter's dwelling of grey stone, with a slate roof and small deep-sunk windows. I jumped out of the car and stood gazing at the expanse of grey-blue sea, set with islands like jewels. There were mountains far out to sea, probably on a finger of the mainland to the south. They were pink quartz in colour and as the clouds went across the sky, they changed to blues and greens and purples and golds. It was a painter's paradise. The gulls went wheeling over our heads, swooping down closely to look at us and then gliding away out and sideways, effortlessly over the ocean, which glittered far below our feet.

There were sheep on the green hills, that ran up behind the cottage and the bracken of the mountains in the background blazed in the sunlight of the calm bright evening. A stream came down the hills, running along from waterfall to waterfall, to end its life in a long skein of white wool, as it fell to the sea.

"My God! She was right," I exclaimed. "This is an enchanted place."

"You'd better wait till you see the inside," Westlake said gloomily, taking a great old key from the pocket of his jacket. "It's probably primitive. It's bound to be."

"There's been no time to get much done to it," I told him. "It's a new toy of Ophelia's. There are plans afoot to put in a plate glass window instead of the front wall, and run the door in at the side, but it would look out of place in this setting. I like it as it is. I can't see it modernised in any way. Besides think what the winter storms might make of a window of any size on this cliff."

He turned the key in the lock with some difficulty and

pushed back the front door. It complained rustily on its
hinges and a shower of earwigs descended on his head,
and made him step back quickly and brush frantically at
his hair. I walked past him into the living room and was
surprised at its spaciousness. The original central passage
and two rooms had been knocked into one and there was
a small lean-to kitchen built onto the back. I went over
to admire the open fireplace. The walls of the room were
all rough cut stone, but the mantlepiece had been made
from picked flat pieces of rock presumably collected on
the sea shore below. There was veined white marble and
green Iona marble and rose quartz and pink granite. The
whole effect could not have been bettered. I frowned at
Ophelia's unemptied tarnished brass ash trays and at the
tortoiseshell-framed miniature of myself as Hamlet, Prince
of Denmark, which stood in the place of honour on the
mantlepiece.

The floor was concrete and somebody had put down
cocoa matting. I lifted a corner of this and saw the horrible
collection of dust and sea sand, that had been allowed to
accumulate underneath. The furniture was thick with dust
and the windows wanted cleaning.

"With love from Jonathan" I wrote on the mahogany
surface of the round cottage table, as I had written it on
the miniature, wondering if she realized what an empty
phrase it could be.

There were two slatted chairs on either side of the fireplace and a studio couch piled high with cushions against
the wall. There was a deep comfortable arm chair covered
with faded cretonne and the dust rose in a cloud, when I
struck it with the flat of my hand. I stood looking round
the room. It might have been passable with Mrs. Stewart

in constant attendance, but without domestic help, it was out of the question.

"Mrs. Stewart has not been here since Miss Druce last used it," Westlake explained, still prospecting for earwigs. "It's overdue for a good spring-cleaning, but she's been too ill to see to it. They didn't expect anybody to come up till next summer. You're well out of it, if you want my opinion."

The grate was full of dead ashes, but there was a box of peat by the fireplace and an armful of driftwood, which had probably been carried up from the shore. I went over and looked at the studio picture of Sally, which stood on the deep ledge of one of the windows. The silver frame was black with verdigris and the glass covered with fly specks. Westlake's voice floated out to me from the kitchen.

"Miss Druce doesn't believe in washing dishes."

I looked at the pile of dirty china in the stone sink. She had not bothered to scrape the food off the plates and everything was green mouldy.

"Tir-nan-oge!" I said with heavy sarcasm. "That's the name of the property, and literally translated, it means the land of the young. It's from Gaelic legend . . . a kind of Atlantis. In Tir-nan-oge, everybody is fair and young and beautiful, and there is no ugliness or age or decrepitude. It's the country of the very young . . . a paradise for lovers . . . a place of enchantment."

I picked up a half-smoked cigar from an ashtray and raised an eyebrow at Westlake.

"Not my brand, I assure you," I said drily.

He was holding a frying pan in his hand and he looked at his most disapproving. It was filled with burnt black grease and he threw it down on the draining board with a clatter.

"You cook by oil," he reminded me, and kicked at a twin-burner Beatrice stove with his toe.

I went back into the main room and he followed me and found me looking down at the divan bed.

"And you go to bed by candlelight," he finished. "Not your type of lighting, old man. You couldn't stick this place for three days, even with Mistress Stewart in attendance. You're a product of civilization and there's no such commodity here."

I was watching the light change on the mountains beyond the darkening sea.

"I don't know about that," I said. "It's a wonderfully relaxing place."

"Well it's out of the question without adequate service laid on," he decided voicing my own opinion exactly. "You couldn't cope with looking after yourself here. We can run over in the car and see what the hotel's like. It's twelve miles on the other side of Lismore and we might get you fixed up there. They say it's right on the sea too, but of course, it may well be full of trippers. I could ring up and find out, if you liked."

"I haven't seen a telephone wire since we left the Main Street of Lismore," I observed. "Perhaps you'd better light the fire and send them a smoke signal."

He looked gloomily at the grate.

"You couldn't get that peat going in a hundred years," he said in a weary voice, and I noticed that he was very tired. Foolishly, I remembered my days in the Boy Scouts."

"Nonsense!" I said briskly. "I could get it lit without the slightest difficulty. I'm good at fires."

He looked at me with disbelief written all over his face and I felt irritated that he should consider me to be such a useless sort of person.

"We'll have to camp out here for the night at any rate," I decided. "We're both far too exhausted to go bumping off down that track and start looking for accommodation. I'll get this fire going in a jiffy. You can unpack the stuff from the car."

I scouted round the premises and found plenty of dry kindling and a bundle of newspapers. I could feel Westlake's sarcastic eye on my back, as I knelt down before the grate. I was determined to get the fire going, just to spite him. I packed the paper in and covered it with sticks and then added the driftwood and finally the blocks of peat. I felt a glow of satisfaction at the magnificence of the blaze I created and I turned round to Westlake in ten minutes.

"You've got soot all over your face," he said, dusting the top of the mahogany table with the car duster.

There is not much doubt that he purposely pushed me into the position of not being able to leave Tir-nan-oge. I never knew him to make so many biting remarks about how necessary it was for me to be waited upon hand and foot. He was quite unlike the usual, helpful, self-effacing secretary, that I knew of old. I think he had got it into his head that it might be a good thing for my soul, if I had forty days in the wilderness. I lost my temper with him eventually, as he had intended I should.

"Of course, I can cook," I found myself declaring childishly at one stage, and then I looked at him suspiciously, but he turned his back on me and went off to fill the Beatrice stove with oil. He was back in twenty seconds with the paraffin tin in his hand.

"For one thing, I can't see Jonathan Harley carrying oil all the way from Lismore twice a week. It's just not your part, old man. You know that you'd not put up with it. If I was here to help you, we might manage, but by yourself, it's out of the question."

We had both had two double whiskies by then and I was in a mood to justify myself.

"We'd better wash up all that stuff in the sink," I said. "There's a hook over the fire to hang the black kettle, and there's soap powder and everything else. We can use the table napkins from the picnic basket in the car to dry up, for there's nothing else here, that's clean enough."

"Are you trying to prove something to yourself?" he asked me from the kitchen, but I did not answer him. I drank a cool draught of Old Mull and began to explore the contents of a cupboard in the corner of the room.

"There's all sorts of stuff here," I called out. "Tinned food, beans, bully beef, mayonnaise, salt, pepper, mustard . . . everything you could possibly want."

His voice floated in from the kitchen.

"There's no bread nor potatoes."

"So I can't cook for myself?" I demanded pettishly. "Good God! I lived in a bed-sitter for years. I'm not the spoilt product of Vanity Fair, that you evidently think I am. I would enjoy a Robinson Crusoe existence here. In fact, I've half a mind to try it."

"Stop pulling my leg."

He did not look at me, but came through the room with the black kettle in his hand saying "I suppose I'd better fill this at what the Scots would call the 'bur-r-n."

He was back in two minutes with muddy shoes, to

hang the kettle over the fire, where it presently began to sing in a most restful manner.

"Of course, if people knew who you were, you could live like a king," he said thoughtfully. "The holiday makers would come out in droves to view the great Jonathan Harley in his new part as Robinson Crusoe and they would provide you with cakes and ale."

I looked at him coldly.

"The point of the whole trip is that I remain anonymous. I'm trying to get away from humanity. Have you forgotten that? I don't want the place buzzing with sight-seers and I don't want their blasted cakes and ale."

He shook his head sorrowfully and poured out fresh drinks for us both, coming over to put mine into my hand and somehow making me conscious that he was still waiting upon me.

"I'm sure that you could do it, if you were pushed," he said. "But you're not pushed. We'll get back to town tomorrow or the next day and you'll see that Tir-nan-oge was just a pipe-dream."

I was not so sure that I was not being pushed and pushed very hard at that.

"Miss Druce is in town by now," he reminded my. "She'll be glad to have you back to squire her to all the parties."

"Don't you know it was to escape . . . " I began and stopped short.

I drained my whisky in one gulp.

"It's not so good without the ice," he said and kicked at the peat on the fire with his toe, while I scowled at his back.

"I've decided to stay on here," I said. "Mrs. Stewart or no Mrs. Stewart."

He spun round and pretended to be dismayed.

"Oh, no!" he cried. "It's quite impossible. You couldn't stick it for six days, let alone six weeks. Please don't make such a hasty decision. It wouldn't do, J.H.! It just wouldn't work out."

"I will remain here for six weeks," I declared, over-confident from the effects of too much whisky.

"Of course, if we could get somebody to replace Mrs. Stewart . . . " he said slowly and I fell into his trap.

"I want nobody to replace Mrs. Stewart," I said hotly. "Good God! Do you think I can't rough it? Do you think that I'm a pampered and spoilt Lord Fauntleroy? Do you think I can't get along without you and my daily woman and old Bill, my dresser, and Uncle Tom Cobley and all? I'll stay out of circulation for six weeks and what's more, we'll have a bet on it."

We argued all the evening and he pushed me more and more firmly into the part that he wanted me to play. We washed up Ophelia's stacked dishes and we dusted the furniture. Westlake even took up the matting and swept the dust into a small heap by the door. We found some silver polish and he got a fine shine on the frame of Ophelia's portrait. He held it out to me several times to emphasize his arguments and once he looked at it thoughtfully for a long time.

"I won't let her chase you up," he said suddenly. "I'll be in town and I'll get wind of it, if she turns her face in this direction. I'll send you a wire and you can cut and run."

He looked at me and smiled in his lopsided way. "London's too far away for a smoke signal."

He even made sure that I would not keep the car. We

were sitting very comfortably at a dinner of sliced bully beef and baked beans, with a bottle of Chateau Neuf du Pape, and by then we had lit two candles and put them on the table. He had polished the brass candlesticks to perfection and he looked at the small flames through the ruby of the wine in his glass.

"You'll be all right with the car," he mused, almost to himself. "You must keep that for ferrying supplies back and forth. You'll want it to run over to the hotel for a good meal at night. You'll not be too cut off from gracious living."

"I don't want the car," I said shortly. "You can take it with you. To hell with the car! I'll manage without it."

He laughed so cheerfully that I saw he had got me exactly where he had intended to get me all along, since we had set foot in the cottage. I stood up and took his empty plate from before him and brought it through to the kitchenette.

"There's tinned creamed rice for pudding," I said and plonked a plate of it in front of him. "Do you want it plain or with condensed milk, and will you take brown sugar or white? That's the selection."

I put the two blue sugar bags down one on either side of him and handed him a battered tin spoon, before I went back to sit down.

"I suppose we'd better finish the wine first," I remarked drily. "Even in this savage outpost of civilization, we must conform with tradition."

"So I'm to take the car?" he sighed.

"You'll take the car," I echoed. "And you'll not see me for six weeks. At the end of that time, I'll show up in town as James Hepburn, with a Scots accent and a Spanish beard, all ready to start rehearsals and your wages will be substantially increased, according to the terms of the wager."

"And if you can't stick it out," he said and gave me a grin, that was like no expression that I had ever seen on his face before. "If you can't stick it out, you will seek out the Queen of Scotland and her Company of Strolling Players. You will humble yourself before her and gain her forgiveness and you will appear in person upon the stage at her side, with full publicity and star billing."

I suppose that Westlake must have relented a little during the night. Perhaps he grew doubtful of the wisdom of casting me into the water, when he knew quite well that I could not swim. At any rate, he seemed to be the same old helpful secretary in the morning and he went to a great deal of trouble to see that I was provided with a certain amount of stores. We jolted along the road into Lismore, when we had finished our breakfast of corn-flakes and condensed milk, followed by tinned ham and potato crisps. We washed it down with black instant coffee and he never mentioned the freshly ground coffee beans, we might have had in the flat, or the electric percolator, that switched itself off at the exact moment of perfection. I put on dark glasses and wore an old pair of drill slacks and a high necked sweater and for the first morning, I neglected to shave. I got a certain satisfaction in watching Westlake's efforts with a blunt safety razor, that we found in the cupboard in the shoe cleaning box.

We climbed down the steep path to the sea before breakfast and found a rocky coast. I was disappointed that it was not sandy, but there was a flat rock and a natural swimming bay, where one could swim quite comfortably, if one was careful to avoid the barnacles on getting out again.

The water was like iced champagne and as clear as freshly polished glass. I swam out a hundred yards and was reproved by Westlake, who told me that it was a foolish thing to do in strange waters, as indeed it was.

"You may be able to swim like a fish," he grumbled, as I pulled myself out onto the flat rock. "But you don't know what currents there may be out there. It's tricky with all those islands. Besides, there are sharks in these seas."

He grinned at me.

"Not the sort you're used to, but just as deadly."

"You've grown very cynical all of a sudden," I challenged him. "Last night, it was civilization and now, it's sharks. What have I done to earn all this sarcasm from your tongue?"

"Let's go up to breakfast," he said and stood aside to let me go first up the steep steps, that somebody had cut in the face of the cliff.

It was a very steep climb. I stopped half way up and sat down to get my breath.

"He's fat and scant of breath," quoted Westlake. "Here, Hamlet, take my napkin, rub thy brow."

"What have I done to earn it?" I asked him once more and he sat down with his back to me a few steps down.

I looked out at the pearl grey of the morning islands. The air was heady with salt and fresh with the scent of the sea. There was no sound but the wash of the waves below us and the crying of the gulls above our heads.

"You've earned more gratitude from me, than I've ever been able to tell you," he said suddenly. "My God! Nobody could be kinder than you are . . . nobody could be more sincere . . . more thoughtful for another's trouble. I know that. God! How I know it! We were both struggling in the whirlpool of London at the time and I shut my eyes and clung to your hand."

He was back on the subject of Sheila again. I wondered why he had mentioned her twice recently, when he had not spoken of her for years.

"I clung to your hand and you took me up through the blackness. You took me up with you on your rocketing career. I'm a man of importance now, even if I'm in your shadow. People seek me out and ask favours of me, just because I have the ear of the great Jonathan Harley. I wear hand-made shoes and have my suits tailored in Saville Row, and I'm tolerably happy. There's nothing I wouldn't do for you, J.H. You'd only have to ask it. I love you like David loved Jonathan."

I thought he was pulling my leg, for a moment and glanced uncertainly at his back. He was a reticent man. It was very unlike him to come out with such emotional stuff.

"You had the humanities and you loved your neighbour better than you loved yourself. Then you went up to flash like a comet across the skies over London."

I stood up and stretched, feeling embarrassed by his earnestness.

"We'd better go like a Comet up this blasted cliff and have some breakfast," I laughed and ran up the steps ahead of him. I waited for him at the top and we both stood looking out over the sea for a moment.

"I'll finish it for you," I said quietly. "You're trying to tell me that I have filled my coffers with flattery and fame and adulation . . . all spurious coinage. I think that I can pay my debts to my fellows with a signed cheque, which is less in value than a hand on the shoulder and a word in the ear. I've lost the humanities, David, my friend, and you think it's time I found them again. You think it's time I came down to the simple life and supped anchorite's fare. I'm to fast and meditate and come out of it all, re-born. That's it! Isn't it?"

He watched a small ship that was making its way along the coast, three miles off shore.

"I don't know," he said. "I honestly don't know. There's a strange atmosphere about Tir-nan-oge. I got a feeling last night, that a man might be chasing a dream all his life in the rich green meadows and then find it here . . . in solitude and quiet, high up on this hungry plateau above the sea."

"Hungry's the operative word," I laughed. "There's only condensed milk for breakfast. I don't know if you'd prefer your corn-flakes plain. For myself, I'll give it a trial."

Then after breakfast, we had taken the car and set off along the road to Lismore, with me anonymous in dark glasses. The sun was shining and the sheep looked creamy against the green hills. There were small waterfalls all along the way, that tumbled out of the mountains to fling themselves into the sea. As we came in sight of the slate roofs of the town, I looked across at Westlake.

"This can't be the right Lismore, you know," I remarked. "Not the one where those Players were to do their show. There's no theatre and practically no town.

"This is the place all right," he told me. "I asked at the shop last evening. Joshua Mardall plays here for a week every year . . . has done since before the horse trams. It's the big social event of the season."

"But where's the theatre?" I asked him and looked at the crofters' cottages and the neat rows of fishermens' houses. Merciful heavens! There's only one shop."

"I don't know. We can ask at the shop. They're bound to know."

We stood on the bare boards of the General Stores cum Post Office and I looked round at the assortment of goods for sale.

"Ye'll be the gentlemen from Tir-nan-oge?" said the lassie behind the counter. "Dae ye wish the milk drappit off at yer gate in the mornin', when Wullie gaes past wi' the van?"

"Och! That wad suit me very weel, Mistress Jeannie," I said and looked sideways at Westlake.

"My name's no Jeannie," she laughed. "It's Fiona."

"Tis a bonnie name for a bonnie lassie," I said and gave her a bow.

"I think we'd better be getting through our order," Westlake said stiffly and his voice was as foreign as any Frenchman's, against the burr of the girl's soft Highland speech.

He took out a very comprehensive list and went through it in his methodical manner and Fiona eyed me from time to time, as I poked about the shop and chose a few unnecessary luxuries like stuffed olives, tinned smoked salmon and cocktail biscuits, which I supposed they stocked for the caravans passing through.

"Will ye be bidin' lang at Tir-nan-oge?" Fiona asked us, as she helped us load the stuff onto the car.

"Och, no, lassie!" I laughed. "This Sassenach is awa' tae London the day, but I'll be here for a month or mebbe mair. He only cam' by to drap me off on the cliff yonder."

Her teeth were very white and even as she smiled at me.

" 'Tis guid he didna drap ye ower the cliff then. Are yer eyes bad?"

I put up a hand to the thick tortoiseshell frames.

"I was awa' doon tae Edinburgh tae see the doctor," I invented and saw the disapproval in Westlake's back, as he got into the driving seat. "I hae to wear the specks till ma beard grows lang and then mebbe ma eyes will be strong enough to gae withoot."

Westlake started up the engine and trod heavily on the accelerator, and I climbed in beside him and smiled back at the girl.

"I hae a feelin' I've seen ye before noo," she said and wrinkled her brows at me. "Ye're no' on the Telly, are ye?"

Westlake shook his head and drove off and I began to laugh.

"For Pete's sake!" he exclaimed. "What sort of a show do you think you're putting on? It wasn't very funny, you know. I suppose that you did it to amuse me, but that girl was taken with you. She'll probably come out to the cottage on her half day and then what'll you do?"

I leaned back in the seat and stretched my legs out, feeling relaxed and at peace with the world.

"I'll entertain her with bully beef and baked beans and a bottle of Chateau Neuf," I said. "And then she can spring clean the cottage for me and do the washing."

I sat up suddenly.

"My God! The washing! Is there a laundry in the town?"
He looked at me sourly.

"I reckon ye'll dae yer ain," he said. "Misther Robinson Crusoe, and it sairves ye right."

He had one last moment of mercy before he said goodbye after lunch and drove off up the road. He handed me the transistor set from the back seat.

"You'd better have that, J.H. It'll keep you in touch with the world. Goodbye now and good luck! I'll look forward to the rehearsals in six weeks time."

"Mebbe, ye'll hae a rise in yer money, Misther Westlake," I said.

"Mebbe!" he laughed. "It doesn't matter much either way, does it? Not for me. The Queen of Scotland took your mind off your business . . . or perhaps it was the whisky. It was heads I win, tails you lose, with the balance in my favour. You can't come out of it any better off, no matter what you do."

"Come back here, you blasted rogue!" I shouted after him, but he waved a hand at me and I watched the car bump off down the road. I wondered how I could have been so stupid as to have been caught out like that. Of course, he won either way. If I stayed on here, his salary would be increased and if I did not, I must make my apologies to the schoolgirl Portia from the Strolling Players. I closed the white gate carefully and walked back to the cottage and lay on the grass of the plateau at the edge of the cliff, listening to the screaming of the gulls and the washing of the waves far below me. I rolled over onto my face after a bit and watched the sea creep slowly and gently over the rocks at the base of the nearest island. I went asleep very soon and woke in the late evening, feeling chilled and stiff. The sun had gone down and a fresh wind had sprung up. There was a menace to the slate-grey sea and the silent loneliness of the plateau. I went across the grass into the cottage and got the fire blazing up the chimney and then I poured myself out a glass of whisky. I sat in the armchair and took out the script of the new play. After a time, I lit the candles and I read the play straight through from start to finish and tried to feel the atmosphere of it. The wind had risen and it howled down the chimney and I shuddered at the horror of the murder of Riccio and could see him cowering against the skirts of his Royal lady. I could understand the feelings, that Salvage had written into Bothwell. I could feel the love, that this arrogant violent passionate man had felt for his Queen . . . how he could stop at nothing to possess her. I could feel the cold despair in his breast, as her love for him changed to revulsion. I could sense the loneliness of his solitary confinement in the Castle of Dragsholm, and how his mind slipped away, and slipped away, as day succeeded day, and no word came from the Queen, who had divorced him.

Tir-nan-oge was as lonely as any solitary confinement, I thought, when I came to the last shuddering line of Salvage's play. The candlelight made the windows black squares of fear and I wondered if anybody would come up outside and peer in through them. I was glad of Westlake's transistor set. I turned it on and heard the noises of civilization, and the wild savage life, that lived outside the windows, moved back a little. I had an excellent supper of smoked salmon sandwiched between fresh rolls and I drank more whisky, than was good for me. Then I tumbled into bed and slept like a log all the night.

I stuck it out for seven days and at the end of that time, I was very lonely indeed. I had devised many tasks, like Robinson Crusoe, in order that I might alleviate my loss of human companionship. I found the antlers of a deer in the hazel nut grove and fixed them in place over the door, where they looked very fine. I collected all the odd things, which I found thrown up by the sea at high tide and carried them up the cliff . . . wood for the fire, old herring boxes, a ship's door, several glass floats from the fishing nets. I fished from the flat rock and caught a strange assortment of sea-food in this way. I contrived a lobster pot and with beginner's luck, I captured a grey lobster, which looked so fierce and pathetic simultaneously, that I released him at once and let him go about his business. I walked for miles over the hills and collected rams' horns, and then I cut ash sticks and made about half a dozen tolerable walking sticks of which I was very proud indeed.

I met few people in my wanderings, but I stopped and passed the time of day with all of them. I told them a little of my affairs and they told me a little of theirs. I tried to pitch my voice to the lilt and swing of the Highland tongue and I put a hint of it into Bothwell's lines and it made them more effective, when I spoke them aloud, to try to drive solitude back from Tir-nan-oge.

I went into the town every second day to fetch the more perishable stores. At least, I made that excuse to myself, but it was to find somebody to talk to. Fiona disapproved of my stubbly chin, although she was too well-mannered to say it openly, as we talked in a very comradely fashion together.

I tramped back the long miles to the cottage with my tin of paraffin in my hand and my shopping in a knapsack on my shoulders and wondered why on earth I did not give it up and take a train back to town. The loneliness grew almost impossible to bear. I began to seek out human companionship, as a thirsty man seeks out water. I found it more and more difficult to fill in all the empty hours. I would have been happy if Fiona had come out to visit the croft on her half day, just to hear the sound of her voice. I spring-cleaned the cottage, but my efforts were not very good, nor was my household management. I always seemed to forget some item of shopping, when I went to town, and I ran out of the most important things . . . salt, paraffin oil . . . soap flakes . . . small vital things, which seemed very essential in that simple existence. I ran out of soap flakes the day I had decided to attempt my laundry and tried to make do with a cake of harsh red soap. My white polo-necked sweater was quite a different garment, when I took it down from the line, where I had pegged it out to blow in the breeze.

I put it on the next day and got quite a shock, when I saw myself in the long mirror of the General Stores. I had a smudge of soot on the knee of my drill slacks and the sweater was shrunk to absurdity. My stubbled chin gave me a cut-throat appearance, which the dark glasses did nothing to enhance. Fiona shook her head at me.

"Whit hae ye been daeing to yon bonnie Shetland sweater?" she demanded. "Hae ye no lassie to dae yer washin' aifter ye?"

I shook my head mournfully.

"I'd hae bin glad tae dae it for ye mysel', if ye'd thocht fit tae ask me," she said. "But 'tis past praying for noo. 'Twill mebbe fit ain o' yer bairns?"

I wished Westlake was by my side.

"Mebbe!" I said doubtfully. "I'll try it on Wullie."

She looked at me suspiciously.

"Whit part o' Scotland are ye frae?" she asked me. "Ye're no' an Argyll mon."

"I'm frae a wee bit tae the south," I told her and took out my shopping list.

"Border, mebbe?" she suggested. "They talk awfu' queer on the Border."

"Och, no, lassie," I laughed. "That's where a' the marauders cam' frae. I'm no marauder."

"Is yer boss gane awa'?" she asked. "You mon wi' the bonnie big car."

I wished for Westlake's presence more than ever.

"Och aye."

"I think mebbe ye dinna work for him noo?" she pursued. "Did ye get the push?"

I bent my head and looked at the floor and made no answer to her.

"Never mind!" she comforted me. "There's mair fesh in the sea, and he was a mean lookin' old deil. I'd no like to work for a mon, who could nae laugh at a joke."

"A joke?"

"Och aye. That first day, when ye baith cam' here and ye called me Mistress Jeannie. He was mad at ye, for makin' so free wi' a lassie. Was that why he give ye the push?"

I told her that I had better get my shopping done and she was very sympathetic with me. She packed the stuff into the haversack and helped me to sling it on my shoulders.

q "Yon garment is in a tarrible way," she sighed. "Yer wife will be mad at ye."

I picked up my can of paraffin from the counter.

"Mebbe she wud!" I laughed. "If I had a wife, but I havena."

"And who's Wullie then?"

I went off through the shop door laughing back at her over my shoulder and the bell jangled harshly.

"Wullie is a figment o' my imagination," I said. "He only exists in ma heid."

She followed me out to the street and stood with her hands on her hips.

"Are ye daft or whit?" she demanded. "How can ye hae a son in yer heid and nae wife? Ye're pullin' ma leig."

Yet it was strange the things that you could have in your head in lovely lonely Tir-nan-oge. I imagined the paradise it could be, if I had a slender dark woman to share it with me. There was a strange elusive quality about it. You could sometimes almost hear the sigh of a woman in your ear . . . see the bright stuff of her gown, as she vanished round the door . . . hear her song in the wind, as it rustled through the nut grove. It was a wild and beautiful country full of romance and splendour.

I sat down on the sea wall and waited for somebody to walk along the road and talk to me and presently I saw a very dilapidated car come chugging towards me. It was a baby Austin of ancient vintage, but it was unlike any car of its make that I had ever seen, for it was painted a bright yellow and the spokes of the wheels were brilliant scarlet. It was polished till the coachwork shone like glass and it was driven by a woman with a square pleasant face and brown hair. She stopped fifty yards down the street from me and opened the door. I was amazed when she stepped from behind the wheel, for she was a dwarf. Her face and her body seemed to be perfectly normal, but her legs and her arms were foreshortened to a grotesque degree, and she was not more than three and a half feet in height. She paid no attention to me, but leaned into the back of the car and took out a step-ladder, which she set up by the wall, that bordered the road. She then marched in a very business-like manner back to the car and this time, she extracted a bucket, which she put by the ladder. Last of all, she fetched a bundle of posters.

She climbed the ladder nimbly and without the least self-consciousness, began to post her bills with wonderful efficiency. I could not read the print from where I sat and I thought it more tactful to wait till she had gone, although I would have been glad to talk to her. I argued that she was probably rather sensitive about her size and that she would be shy with strangers, so I pretended I was not watching her and looked at the wall opposite where I sat.

The sea was at my back and the waves were hurling the small stones against the beach with a scrunching noise, for it was a windy rough day. I heard her cry of distress from where I sat and looked back towards the car. Two of the posters had been torn from her grasp and were blowing down the road towards me. I stood up and went across to retrieve them for her, but one evaded me and soared up into the air like a kite. I waved my hand at her.

"Don't worry. I'll get it for you."

I pinned it with my stick against the grass of the bank two hundred yards away, after a breathless chase and looked down to see what it said.

There was a picture of a handsome white-haired man in the centre of it and I read the words printed above and below.

JOSHUA MARDALL'S COMPANY OF STROLLING PLAYERS
JOSHUA MARDALL HAS GREAT PLEASURE IN ANNOUNCING
THE FIRST APPEARANCE UPON THE STAGE OF ANY THEATRE

of

JULIET HEMINGWAY
WHO WILL PLAY PORTIA IN SCENES FROM
THE MERCHANT OF VENICE
IN THE PARISH HALL OF LISMORE, NEXT WEEK, NIGHTLY AT
EIGHT O'CLOCK PRECISELY (except Suns.)
WITH JOSHUA MARDALL HIMSELF AS
SHYLOCK, THE JEW,
SUPPORTED BY THE FULL COMPANY.
The Show will be opened by a performance of
THE SPANISH LADY, A ONE ACT PLAY,
BY JOSHUA MARDALL
(which has been requested by many patrons)

I bent down and picked up the poster and rolled it carefully with the one I had already retrieved. Then I retraced my steps in a more orderly fashion along the road towards the car. The little woman had come down the ladder and was waiting for me. The top of her head was on a level with my waist. I smiled at her.

"It's amazing how the wind can take this sort of thing," I remarked. "It was lucky they didn't end up in the sea."

She thanked me and began to go back up the steps, but

I put a hand on her shoulder.

"It's a bit too stormy today. Don't you think you'd better let me put up the rest of them? I have nothing else to do and I'd be glad to have somebody to pass the time of day with."

She thanked me very graciously and instructed me in the art of bill-sticking, and I did not make too much a mess of it, though I was not as adept as she was, by a long shot.

"Hermione Kiddle," she said, when we had finished. "I belong to the Players. I'm wardrobe mistress, and secretary and treasurer and a lot of other things besides. Jill of all trades and mistress of none. That's Hermione Kiddle."

"How do you do, Miss Kiddle." I said and shook her hand ceremoniously, although we were both sticky with paste by then.

"I'm John . . . . "

I pulled myself up short and there was a pause of about ten seconds, while I searched frantically about for a name, but could think of none.

"I'm John," I finished lamely. "I'm not particularly fond of my second name. Just call me John."

She looked at me intently for a second and then turned away again towards the sea.

"I suppose we'd better go and rinse our hands," she suggested. "I have to give Dog Toby a run on the beach in any case."

She went over to the car and I saw that she had a hassock to sit on and special controls for her short legs. There was a dog, sitting on the seat next hers, in a most dejected begging posture, with his ears at half cock and his tail wagging a little. She opened the door and he jumped down and ran to sniff at a concrete post. Then he came and sat on his haunches again and showed the whites of his eyes at me in his dismal fashion. I squatted down beside him and stroked his head and the small lady laughed all over her face.

"He wants to be properly introduced," she told me. "He's Dog Toby in the Punch and Judy Show. You must shake hands with him."

"Dog Toby, this is Mr. John. Mr. John, this is Dog Toby."

I took his fluffy paw in my hand with great gravity and he was satisfied and trotted off down onto the beach, where I was pleased to throw sticks for him, after we had got the paste off our hands at the tide's edge. He was a little white dog with long silky hair and he looked like a bundle of rags, as he bounded along the shingle. Miss Kiddle sighed, as he retrieved a stick from the water and came back to us with his hair clinging about his body.

"You wouldn't believe the difference the ruff makes to him. You'd die with laughter, if you could see all his tricks. He's one of the cleverest dogs on the stage today. There's nothing he can't do."

"Is he on the stage as well as in the Punch and Judy Show?" I asked her, coming back to where she had pulled herself up to sit on a concrete slab with her small legs dangling.

"Oh, yes! He used to come on with the players in Hamlet, when we had the full company, and he was in the circus with me, before he took to Punch and Judy."

"So you have a Punch and Judy Show with the Strolling Players?"

I offered her a cigarette, which she took and put between her lips. I bent down and lit it with my gold lighter and I saw her eye take in the incongruity of such an opulent affair being in my disreputable possession.

"Don't you think I'm big enough to smoke?" she laughed, and yet I knew that she forced herself to joke at her small stature . . . that really she was sensitive and shy about it, and miserable because she was a normal being enclosed in a dwarf's body. I was very sorry for her suddenly and wondered what to say to make her feel any better about it.

"I should think you know your own mind," I said. "You seem a most capable lady to me, and you haven't told me about the Punch and Judy Show yet.

She inhaled a deep breath of smoke and blew it out towards the sea and the wind took it from her mouth and made nothing of it and lifted the brown hair from her forehead.

"Samuel Barldrop does the Punch and Judy. Meggie is his wife and she's by way of being a fortune teller . . . very good at it, she is too. She can do a wonderful horoscope. . . better than anybody I ever met. Of course, they take part in the legitimate stage too. Everybody does except me. Their son is Cedric and he's the juvenile lead. He's Bassanio next week. Apryl's their daughter and she's Nerissa. You can see them all in the Merchant."

"And Joshua Mardall is to play Shylock?" I put in and sat down at her feet to lean my back against the concrete slab.

"Joshua Mardall is the whole show," she said and her voice was so full of admiration and reverence, that I turned to look up at her. Her face was lit up by her love for him.

"Mr. Mardall is one of the best producers and play-wrights in the country," she sighed and looked back at the car, which was a hundred yards away on the road. "Would you like a cup of coffee and a sandwich?" she asked me. "You don't look as though you've had a square meal for a long time."

I looked down at the stones between my feet and nodded my head and she told me that she had a picnic lunch in her car. She allowed me to fetch it for her and I was very touched at the way she divided her meagre rations equally between us. She had a bone wrapped in newspaper for Dog Toby and he sat up and begged for it and took it away behind a rock growling most fiercely, as if he feared I was going to take it away from him.

"Mr. Mardall is the kindest person in the world," she declared, sipping her coffee daintily from the top of the Thermos. She had given me the cup, and I held it between my hands and gazed out over the sea.

"I think that perhaps you're a very kind person yourself," I said. "You're feeding a complete stranger, aren't you?"

"We must all help each other," she said and took a bite from her paste sandwich, which she munched for a while before she went on.

"You're in some sort of trouble, aren't you? You don't add up . . . not one little bit. You won't tell me your name and you're dressed in rags and tatters, and yet you have an expensive cigarette lighter."

She tapped me on the top of the head with a stick she had picked up from the shore. I was sitting at her feet again by now with my back against the concrete.

"I'm not saying you stole it. You haven't got the eyes of a thief. It's yours all right and yet you're down on your luck. I suppose you wouldn't like to tell me what's the matter. A trouble shared is a trouble halved."

I shook my head.

"I'm not in any difficulty."

"That's what we all say," she sighed.

I had finished my sandwich and drunk my coffee, before she spoke again.

"Joshua Mardall could help you."

I turned round and looked up at her in surprise.

"Joshua Mardall?"

She bent down towards me and swung her small legs in their absurd strapped children's shoes.

"Your eyes are the same colour as the sea," she remarked. "Green and deep and beautiful. You'd be better without that beard."

I put my sun-glasses on quickly and cursed myself for having taken them off, when I chased the posters.

"You are in trouble," she said. "You're hiding out from something. Come now. Confess it."

I looked down at the ground between my knees and said nothing.

"I think I'd better tell you about Mr. Mardall," she said. "Then you can decide. I don't often talk about it, but I can see that there's something very wrong with you, and we might put it right between us."

She scrambled down from the slab and began to throw the stick for Dog Toby and I walked along beside her, with her Thermos flask under one arm and my hands in my pockets.

"Have you ever seen dwarfs in a circus?" she asked me at last, turning round to face me and looking up at my face. "And take those stupid glasses off. I want to see your eyes."

I did as she commanded and stood in front of her a

little helplessly.

"Have you?" she said again and I nodded my head.

"I was a dwarf in a circus. It may be all right for some, but it wasn't for me. We were a funny act and we made people laugh and that was all there was to it."

She put her fists on her hips.

"Do you know what it's like to be laughed at, day after day, night after night, week after week, year after year . . . just for being the way God thought fit to make you . . . when inside your heart, you are the same as the fools who laugh at you?"

I squatted down to bring my face level with hers.

"I can believe that might be very great trouble indeed," I said and my voice was husky with the pain I felt in my breast for her. I took one of her hands in mine and I smiled at her.

"It was an infernal impudence of anybody who laughed at you. I find nothing amusing in the way God made you. You're one of the most charming companions I have ever met and you're a creature of great humanity besides. For all you know, I might be a blackguard of the worst sort, yet you shared your lunch with me, because you saw I was in trouble."

"So you are in trouble," she cried triumphantly. "There's something familiar about you. I've seen a picture of you without that beard on your face, and I know your voice too. I've met you somewhere before, but I can't for the life of me remember where . . . . "

"You were telling me about the circus," I reminded her.

"Joshua Mardall is a man like you . . . a man of perception," she said. "He saw the show one night and he came to my caravan afterwards. I was a bit low. Usually I managed to let people think I didn't care, but this night . . . oh, well, it doesn't matter. I suppose my eyes were red, but he knew I was down. He told me he wanted somebody to help him with the costumes for the Strolling Players and said he'd heard I was a good needlewoman. He asked *me* to help *him*. He squatted down beside me, like you're doing now and he said that he was at his wits' end."

She laughed suddenly, but she was not far from tears.

"He told me that he couldn't guarantee that I could appear on the stage. I'd work behind the scenes and I'd be more help like that. He said that he could get thousands of people to walk on in a part, but it was difficult to find somebody to do all the work necessary off stage, and not want lime-light."

She sighed and began to walk along the shore, with Dog Toby jumping at her side.

"I told him that I didn't want the lime-light and I'd be glad to go with him and he said to pack my bags at once and join up with his company. Then he gave me a handkerchief to dry my tears."

Her voice was quite fierce with emotion.

"What's more . . . he found the Barldrops down and out at Scarborough. Meggie had pneumonia and they hadn't a penny. He knew Sam from seeing him at the sea-side resorts, and he came on him trying to pawn his coat. Cedric was a small boy at the time and Apryl was a baby in arms and they had nowhere to go. He took them in. He's a good man, Mr. John. Any one of us would die for Joshua Mardall. Don't you think that we'd be glad to help you too?"

She stooped down and picked up the stick and threw it along the shingle and Dog Toby sprang away to retrieve it.

"There's Juliet Hemingway. She's to play Portia next week. It was the same story with Juliet."

I put a hand on her shoulder.

"She's his grandchild," I said almost to myself. "He brought her up since her parents died. She owes him everything too, doesn't she? There's nothing she wouldn't do, if she thought it would help him."

She looked at me in amazement, as well she might and put her hands on her hips again.

"How do you know that?" she asked me. "Who are you? Why do I feel that I've met you before? Why have you left your face unshaven and why do you cover your fine eyes with glasses and hide out from the world?"

"Juliet is tall and regal and slender. Her hair is dark . . . very dark and it comes down on her forehead in a peak. She's not long left school and she's been rehearsing for Portia. She knows her lines well."

She wrinkled her brows at me and I walked back towards the car and threw the stick for Dog Toby again. I helped her up onto the road and opened the car door for her and she climbed nimbly to her hassock and sat looking out at me.

"So you won't let us help you?" she said in a sad little voice.

"I'm not in any trouble. I'll come and see the show next week. Perhaps we'll talk about it again. In the meantime, I thank you for your generosity to me and I assure you that I find you a lady of great charm and distinction."

I picked up one of her small ridiculous hands suddenly on an impulse and bent my head to kiss it.

"I am your humble servant, Miss Hermione Kiddle," I said and walked off down the road to retrieve my can of paraffin and my knapsack, from where I had left them, when I ran to chase the posters.

I walked quickly out along the coast road towards the cottage and thought of my strange encounter with the small lady. I had certainly learned a great deal about the Company of Strolling Players, which I thought sarcastically, went in for Punch and Judy shows on the sands and fortune telling and astrology on the side, presumably to boost funds. At any rate, I would make a point of seeing the show one night, but I knew, before I went, the dreary affair it would be, with the props a little battered and the costumes tawdry and in need of a good laundry.

At this point I pulled down my sweater, which had been gradually working its way up my back, and thought that at least, I was not in much of a position to criticise the laundering of the garments. Still, I knew that old Joshua Mardall would look like Buffalo Bill and would be given to barn-storming melodrama. The juvenile lead . . . what was his name? . . . Cedric . . . Cedric Barldrop would have an adenoidal voice and long hair and suffer from many pimples on his greasy face. I thought of Juliet Hemingway. At least, the name was pretty, but I knew what these dark slender adolescents of the theatre world often turned out to be like, even with raven locks and regal bearing. She might even be given to chewing gum and perhaps to too little fastidiousness. Yet, Westlake had been struck with her and he was very particular about the type of woman, he admired. I was mildly interested to see his "Queen of Scotland" for myself, and I got the chance of it the following Sunday, when the Strolling Players arrived in Lismore.

I had walked into the town to see if I could get some of

the Sunday papers. They came out from Oban by car and the General Stores opened in the afternoon to sell them. The inhabitants of the countryside for miles about congregated outside the shop, some in rather battered Land Rovers or cars, but mostly on foot.

I stood and looked at the poster in the window, which advertised Joshua Mardall's show, before I went in to get my papers. I could see myself reflected in the glass and I thought that at last, the beard was beginning to take shape.

"Och, it's awfu' dear!" said a plaintive voice at my side. "I hae nae siller saved up yet."

There were two schoolboys dressed in their Sunday best, of tartan kilt and too-small tweed jackets.

"Mebbe, the dominie will tak' us frae school. We're daeing the Merchant in class and I'd like weel tae see old Joshua as Shylock. 'Twid be worth the saxpence, and Mistress Kiddle wid na turn ye awa', if she thocht ye had nae money by ye."

"Here they come!" shouted a man in the road and I turned round and saw Hermione Kiddle leading the procession in the Austin, with a middle-aged woman sitting in the passenger's seat, with Dog Toby on her lap. There was a single-decker bus behind the Austin . . . a bus with as much character as Miss Kiddle's vehicle, for it had precisely the same colour scheme, of bright red wheels and yellow coachwork. Along its yellow side, letters a foot high were painted in scarlet to match the wheels;

JOSHUA MARDALL'S COMPANY OF STROLLING PLAYERS

The rack on top of the bus was piled with props of all kinds. At first glance, I took in a bust of William Shakespeare, a great stuffed eagle and a collapsible contraption in striped red-and-white canvas, which obviously belonged to the Punch and Judy Show.

I walked into the shop and stood at the window, pretending to look at a revolving postcard stand, so that I could watch the players dismount. The woman with Miss Kiddle was middle-aged and she was short and full-breasted. She had a round, country dumpling of a face and a small blob of a nose and she was the most motherly person imaginable in her tweed skirt and home-knitted woollens. There was an indefinable cottage-loaf appearance about her.

"You were quite right, Mistress Meggie, 'twas a fine wee laddie . . . eight pound weight."

So that was the fortune teller, I thought, though she looked unlike any fortune teller I had ever seen. The woman, who had shouted to her from the shop doorway went over to talk to her and presently, a short man climbed down from the bus and went to stand by her side. She put out a hand automatically to straighten his tie and then patted his cheek absently. I imagined that he was her husband . . . the Punch and Judy man. He was middle-aged too and stocky, with a rubbery Scots face and sparse fair hair. He had bagpipes under one arm, and he looked gloomy and morose. A girl had jumped lightly from the bus behind him. I knew that she must be Juliet Hemingway, for she was young and dark, but of course, she did not come up to Westlake's description of her. She was certainly a strange sight to see in the West of Scotland. She would have been far more at home in a School of Ballet. She wore a man's sweater with a high neck . . . black to match her black tights and flat black pumps. A cascade of bracelets winked and glittered at her wrist and caught her eye. Her hair was divided in the centre of her head and dressed low on the nape of her neck in a bun.

She moved langurously and she was pretending to be very bored with the whole proceeding, but she was conscious of the effect she was having on the youth of the countryside, who looked at her with their mouths dropping open.

"If I were gang oot like yon," said Fiona from behind the counter, voicing the feelings of all the women in the shop. "Ma mither wid skelp me till I couldna sit doon for a week."

The dark motherly woman stretched her arms out from her sides, as if she was calling her children to come to her and several of the women went over to her to form an animated group. The girl had collected a bunch of fair-headed curly haired youths in kilts, who were behaving skittishly and inclined to turn to horseplay among themselves to hide their emotions. She was not as dark as I had supposed, but she certainly seemed to have a high opinion of her charms. I thought of the way I had intended to seek her out and apologize and I decided firmly that I would do no such thing. She would think I was trying to flirt with her, and she looked just as tenacious as Ophelia. I cursed Westlake for his false description of her. Scotland would be a sorry place, if it possessed such a Queen. She twined her arm through that of the most personable boy present and his face was the colour of a beetroot, with mingled pleasure and embarrassment.

Who did Westlake think I was, that I should apologize to a girl of this type? She had just made a fool of him and I had shown correct judgment from start to finish in turning her from my door. She started to giggle in a most inane and foolish manner, that made every middle-aged woman in her vicinity long to box her ears.

I went across to the counter and bought my papers and

Fiona was so interested in the arrival of the Players, that she did not even look at me. She served me absent-mindedly and smiled over my shoulder at the scene outside.

"Och, Mr. Mardall!" she cried, as I picked up my change. "Welcome back tae Lismore! We're a' that excited aboot Juliet starting her career. She's the bonniest lassie in the whole country and she'll dae fine as Portia."

I did not think much of her opinion. I tucked the papers under my arm and decided to make myself scarce, but a tall, elderly man blocked my way through the door. He was a most distinguished looking old chap with longish, silvery hair and jutting white brows. He held himself like a guardsman, and if he had been dressed in tweeds, he would have looked like a retired brigadier. As it was, his shabby velvet jacket and his flowing tie hinted that he belonged to my own profession. I got an impression of shabby shoes, polished to perfection and trousers frayed at the ends, but with knife edge creases, beautiful hands, graceful theatrical gestures, lines of good humour, crow's-footed about his eyes.

"Mistress Fiona!" he cried in a deep pleasant voice. "It gives me pleasure to greet you again . . . exquisite jewel that you are, in an exquisite setting. I thought that some Highland chieftain would have carried you off to his castle in the hills ere now."

I stood aside to let him come into the shop and then went out into the street. The inhabitants of Lismore were certainly giving the Players a great reception. There were no press photographers or reporters, but each member of the troupe was surrounded by a group of friends, and the rubbery-faced man was marching up and down with his bagpipes, filling the air with the strains of "Highland

Laddie." It was clear that the company had been here many times before, and that they were very popular indeed.

Nobody even turned a head to look at me, as I walked along the path and I felt strangely put out about it. I had grown accustomed to being the centre of attraction where-ever I went, and although I had thought that this irked me, I felt rather hard done by and rather sorry for myself, as I walked off along the cliff road to my lonely cottage, with-out a soul to care whether I came or went.

An old Hillman car had parked behind the bus . . . a square old car of a shape, that would have looked more at home following a funeral. I classed it as a 1928 model, but I may have been a year or two out either way. The colour, at any rate, would have been most unsuitable for a mourning procession, for it had been painted yellow and red to match the rest of the entourage. I glanced at it curiously as I went by and saw the school trunk, that stood up-ended in the back with the initials J.R.H. It might have been Miss Hemingway's property, I mused. Presumably the old man would have sent her to a boarding school to insure that she got a better education than would have been possible, if she had accompanied the Strolling Players on tour. The back seat of the car was piled high with luggage of all descriptions, and rugs and coats and books and papers and gloves and bars of chocolate and all the paraphenalia of a motoring trip.

I walked on and thought of Juliet Hemingway with her black tights and fisherman's jersey and her circle of infatuated country bumpkins. My lip curled a little as I thought what she would make of Portia. I passed the row of houses, that were built in a terrace beside the General

Stores, and there was a wall, that hid the front path of
the last house of all. I heard footsteps come running down
the flagstones, but I had no time to avoid the inevitable
collision. I got a glimpse of flying black hair and the
swing of a tartan skirt, as a young girl took me in the
chest with the point of her shoulder and sent me staggering
across the pavement towards the road. I put up my hands
and grabbed at her and tried to prevent her falling and she
clutched at me instinctively and knocked my dark
spectacles off my nose onto the pavement, with a tinkle
of splintering glass. She stayed in my arms for five
seconds, too startled to move and then she pulled herself
free and looked down at the broken glasses. Her face filled
with dismay and she bent quickly to pick up the empty
frames, before she raised her eyes to mine.

"Oh, dear! Now look what I've done."

I took the wretched things out of her hand and threw
them away and she held her right shoulder with her left
hand and stood biting her lip and looking up at me in
dismay, as I kicked the broken fragments of glass into
the gutter.

"You're in a great hurry," I frowned at her. "If you're
trying to catch the great Joshua Mardall to ask for his
autograph, you have plenty of time. His Company will be
here all the week, and I daresay he'll find occasion to sign
your book, if you smile at him and ask him nicely."

"Joshua Mardall!" she said breathlessly. "Joshua
Mardall!"

"He's only just arrived," I said with an edge of sarcasm
in my voice. "You haven't missed anything much. His
highly coloured circus has drawn up outside the General
Stores, and you'll find him in the shop, flirting with Fiona

McLeod, who seems very taken with him."

"Fiona McLeod!" she said still clasping her shoulder. "So Fiona McLeod is taken with him?"

I smiled at her, but she did not seem to be very friendly.

"I expect you know her," I remarked. "You live here, don't you?"

"I know her very well," she answered.

She seemed to echo everything I said and I thought that she did not like me very much.

"Are you going to the show?" I asked her to make conversation and she nodded her head and her dark hair swung about her face.

She was very beautiful. Her eyes were set wide apart and were very deep blue and her lashes swept her cheeks. Her face was classic in its loveliness . . . her nose straight, her eyebrows slanting up and out, her hair coming down in a peak on her forehead.

"Did you see them playing last year?" I went on and she nodded her head and did not speak.

"Are they worth going to see?" I pursued. "Or is it the usual moth-eaten sea-side show . . . travelling pierrots and that sort of thing?"

I laughed and went on.

"Does Punch and Judy have a show on the foreshore for the benefit of the children?"

She did not even smile at me, but looked back towards the shop.

"Have you had Meggie What's-her-name tell your fortune?" I asked her, feeling rather ashamed of myself by now. "And did she tell you that you were going to meet a dark stranger and break his glasses for him?"

"Meggie Barldrop," she corrected me and bit her

lip again.

She went over to look down at the broken frames and her brow was furrowed.

"I'm sorry about those. I should get them mended for you. It was my fault. They look very good ones too. I expect they cost you a lot."

I laughed and told her to forget the damage to my spectacles.

"Tell me about the Show." I prompted her. "I'm far more interested in that."

She clasped her hands behind her back and swung her kilted skirt back and forth like a little girl.

"Are they worth seeing?"

She looked up into my face, as if she disliked me very much indeed and then she laughed suddenly. It was as if the sun glinted on the deep clear waters of the ocean. Her teeth were white and even and the dimples came and went beside her red mouth.

"I'm very much afraid that it mightn't meet with your Majesty's approval," she said and silver fishes of fun swam in her eyes. "I expect you're accustomed to the Old Vic and Stratford-upon-Avon. It's not really quite as good as that, but the people here like it. Their tastes are very simple."

She was very much in defence of Joshua Mardall and his Company of Strolling Players. She was angry with me for being so high and mighty and she was in the right . . . not I, as well I knew.

She put her hands deep into the pockets of her jumper and raised a brow at me.

"I suppose that you'd consider the production 'moth-eaten'," she said with an edge to her voice. "They do realize that they fall short and they don't claim to be all that wonderful."

> "A substitute shines brightly as a king
> Until a king be by . . . . "

She dropped me a little curtsey and finished "Your Majesty."

The words hit me between the eyes, like a physical blow. I wondered how I could have been such a tactless blundering idiot. I had been piqued because nobody had paid homage to me and had said a lot of senseless things. The dark hair on her forehead in a peak, the slender body, the thin shoulders and now this quotation from her lines . . . Portia's lines . . . it added up to one thing and one thing only. She was Juliet Hemingway. I put out a despairing hand and grasped her shoulder. I turned her round to face the crowd outside the shop door.

"Who is the dark girl in the black sweater?"

"That's Apryl Barldrop. The piper is her father and Meggie is her mother. Meggie's the dark lady by the door. She's marvellous."

I sat down abruptly on the stone wall, which edged the front garden of the house.

"My God!" I said and again "My God! You're Juliet Hemingway . . . I thought you lived in that house. I thought you were rushing out to . . . I wouldn't have said all that nonsense . . . . "

I stood up again and looked down at her and cursed myself for my boorishness, but she was staring up the road and her face was sad. I was horrified to see that suddenly, she was not far from tears.

"I suppose they *are* bad," she said almost to herself. "So much the more reason for not deserting them."

A boy of her own age was running along the path towards us. He had jumped out of the driving seat of the bus, when they had arrived, so I took him for the son of the Punch-and-Judy man, Barldrop, that Miss Kiddle had told me about. He was clad in tight blue jeans and he wore a black shirt. His fair hair was too long, but he had a happy laughing face. Dog Toby was running at his heels and barking in a hysterical fashion. The boy took no notice of me, but grabbed Juliet by the hand.

"Come on, Juliet! Where did you get to? We're all waiting for you. The McLeod's have tea for us and the old man is fretting in case you've gone and drowned yourself in the sea."

He dragged her off along the path and the dog circled them, jumping up and down in his raggedy-mop fashion. She looked back at me over her shoulder.

"Sorry about your Majesty's spectacles. Come and judge the Show for yourself. Goodbye now!"

They ran off together and I stood there and watched them and felt old and lonely and locked out. I had two apologies to make now instead of one, and of course, she was all that Westlake had said of her. She was youth and light and joy and grace and beauty.

A great rough-looking old Scot in a tartan kilt put his arms about her, as she drew abreast of him at the shop door. He kissed her very heartily and she put her arms up about his neck. He swung her round and round and his kilt and her skirt made a bright carousel of colour. I turned on my heel and went off along the coast road and wondered what on earth had come over me that I envied him so much. I recalled the few moments, when I had held her in my arms . . . held her tightly against my chest. I remembered the way her hair had been fragrant and fresh, and I cursed myself for the things I had said about her miserable Company of Strolling Players, but there seemed very little to be done about it at that moment.

It came on to rain in a light Scots mist, that was very deceptive. I was soaked to the skin, by the time I got to the cottage and the fire had gone out. It took me an hour to get it going again, because I had not laid in any dry wood. Eventually, I put most of my paraffin oil onto the peat and almost succeeded in burning down the whole building. Then I found that I had left myself no oil for the cooking stove, so I had to cook as best I could on the open fire on the hearth. I managed to get my supper impregnated with paraffin and my person too. I was in a savage humour by the time I sat down and picked up my script, and then she came walking down the avenues of my imagination . . . dressed in a starched high Medici collar, her coif very white against her dark hair . . . a perfect Mary, Queen of Scotland . . . regal and slender and gracious.

I was very hot and feverish by the time I went to bed, and I knew I was in for a cold. I slept an uneasy sleep, full of strange dreams and she was in every one of them, but always she hated me . . . always she turned away from me in revulsion, till my whole being was full of such despair and misery, as I had never known before.

I woke up in the morning with a heavy chill, still feeling a trace of the misery of my dreams of the night. My throat was sore and I ached all over. I had a harsh dry cough, which hurt my side. I felt disinclined to walk into Lismore to fetch the paraffin, so I had to make do on the open fire for my cooking, and as usual, I was not very successful about it.

I was very little better over the next few days and the weather set in very wet and cold. The grey mist hid all the beauty and splendour of the mountains round about, and the sheep huddled together miserably in front of the cottage, with their witches' eyes, asking why on earth I was fool enough to stay in this forlorn comfortless place. The trees were dismal and dripped rain incessantly and the burns were full to overflowing, cascading their water-falls down the hills in skeins of white wool. Everywhere was the sound of water . . . dripping, splashing, plashing, cascading, rushing, gushing, and it went on day after day.

It was not until Saturday that the sun came out again and I felt up to the long tramp into town. I had a swim in the sea and got into a pair of cavalry twill slacks and a fresh shirt and sweater. I was pleased when I looked at myself in the glass and saw how the beard had come on. I shaped it neatly with a razor, that I had bought in the Stores. I got it in a line along my jaw and tufted out a bit at the chin and I thought that in a week or two, it would be just as I had planned it.

It was very cold after the swim and I put on a corduroy jacket over the heavy green sweater. The jacket was a favourite relaxing garment of mine, for all its age. Even without my dark glasses, I was a very different looking fellow from Jonathan Harley, and I had not much to fear being recognized, as I tramped along the twisting track to Lismore.

A woman in a Land Rover gave me a lift after I had gone half a mile and I was very thankful for it too, She looked at me, as she dropped me off at the Stores and told me that my face was vaguely familiar, though she could not place it.

"You're probably confusing me with somebody else," I said. "All bearded men look alike and mine is a very ordinary type of face."

She was a stout middle-aged woman, clad in good tweeds, with a hand-knitted cardigan over her spotless silk blouse. She looked at me, as I stood beside the car and laughed all over her jolly face.

"So you consider that you've got an ordinary kind of face?" she said. "Och, laddie, you've got a face that'll break all the lassies' hearts for miles around. If I was twenty years younger and not old enough to be your mother, I'd not put you out in Lismore. I can tell you that."

She drove off before I could think of any reply, and I went into the shop to talk to Fiona McLeod.

"I thocht ye'd gane awa'," she cried.

I told her that I'd had a cold and I went through the shopping list with her. She packed the things neatly into my haversack for me and put the paraffin tin on the counter.

"I'll be awa' hame then," I sighed and she looked at me in surprise.

"Are ye no' stayin' tae see the Players?" she asked me. "They're awfu' guid. Juliet Hemingway's a wonderful actress, and Cedric wid mak' ye dee laughin' as Bassanio."

I refrained from telling her that the part of Bassanio was in no way a comic one, but I gave her a sarcastic look all the same.

"You've seen the Show then?"

"Och, aye. I see it every night. Whit else is there tae dae in Lismore?"

"It's a lang road back to Tir-nan-oge," I said doubtfully, resuming my Scots accent.

"I cud ask Jamie Stewart tae gie ye a lift in his jaloppy," she told me and I smiled at the American influence of the cinema. "He'll be in for sure and he gaes hame right by yer gate. He's got a crush on Apryl Barldrop, but she's a tarrible flirt, and he's wastin' his time."

"That's the wee lassie wi' the bun o' hair on the back o' her neck?" I asked her. "I didna think much tae her."

She looked at me approvingly.

"That's richt!" she nodded. "She hae a' the laddies driven daft wi' those black trews o' hers. Wid ye no' think shame tae gang roun' in yon?"

I smiled to myself and told her that I would and she liked me better than ever.

"A skelpin' on the seat o' her trews wid na dae her ony hairm," she pondered. "But Jamie Stewart is no' the mon tae dae it. Still I'll introduce ye tae him, if ye like tae come back at half seven. He'll gie ye a lift and welcome."

I walked round the town for a bit and went to look at the Parish Hall, which was the theatre. It was an ugly stone building with four steps up to the front door. The Playbill was posted on the board outside and I saw again that the entertainment would be opened by a one-act play, called the Spanish Lady, starring Apryl Barldrop and Cedric Barldrop, which would be followed by extracts from the Merchant of Venice with Juliet Hemingway as Portia. A gala performance would be given every night in honour of Miss Hemingway's debut as a leading player on any stage in the United Kingdom.

I wandered down to the sea front and saw that the Punch and Judy Show was in full swing, watched by a handful of children on their way home from school. I sat on a bollard at a little distance, and presently a few sturdy Scotswomen came up and joined the audience, with their shopping baskets on their arms.

My friend, Dog Toby, with rather a bedraggled frill about his feathery neck, was sitting mournfully up front in his traditional position, and his ears were at half cock, because of the dreadful boredom of it all.

Samuel Barldrop was excellent. He gave the age-old performance admirably and the children loved him, but they did not notice the shabbiness of the whole set-out, nor yet the beaten look in Barldrop's eyes, when he came round with the hat after the show. He did not even bother to ask the children for money. They ran off along the shore with no word of thanks and he came over to his adult audience and managed to seem apologetic about asking for payment at all. He left me to the last and was surprised when I dropped a fifty new pence piece into his cap. I estimated his takings at very little indeed.

"Thank you kindly, sir," he said. "That's mighty generous of you."

"Nonsense!" I told him with a smile. "That was a very excellent and enjoyable performance you gave us. Do you know that Punchinello has played in England for over three hundred years? Everybody likes Mr. Punch. He'll run for ever."

I went across to the box and shook hands with Dog

Toby and then I lifted him down from his high perch, for he was tired of it all. Barldrop stooped to untie the frill from about his neck and told him that he was a very good dog. He awarded him with a lump of sugar, which he balanced on the dog's nose to entertain me, with the old trick of "On trust" and "Paid for."

"Things are not as good as they used to be," I prompted Samuel, and he looked at me for a moment as he folded the dog's frill and put it carefully away.

"I don't complain none," he said. "You still get the bairns' laughter and it's better than any money could ever be. That'll not change with the times. They still love to see old Punch beating his wife and baby and coming out on top of the devil in the end. The day they don't laugh at old Mr. Punch . . . that's the day things will not be so good, but I reckon it won't come yet a while."

He packed up all his props with great care and I wished him good luck. He went off to the shop and I passed the window in a minute or so, and saw him buying stores, presumably with the money he had earned . . . bread and a pint carton of milk and a small packet of tea. I imagined that the Strolling Players worked on a very narrow margin of profit and felt sorry for my fellow entertainers. I wished that I had put more money in his hat, but there seemed nothing I could do about it at this stage. I walked along the edge of the sea and thought uncomfortably of Juliet's eyes as she had said "I suppose they are bad. So much the more reason not to desert them." I tried to tell myself that it was none of my business, and then remembered Donne and how "no man is an island . . . when the bell tolls it tolls for thee."

I went back to the stores eventually and was formally

introduced to Jamie Stewart and he said that he would be delighted to give me a lift home after the show. I stayed to chat with Fiona for a while and at ten minutes to eight, I strolled across to the Parish Hall and mounted the steps to the front door. It was different from any theatre I had ever come across. It was illuminated by a single bare bulb over the door and there were no milling crowds, no orderly queues, no buskers, nor anything else remotely connected with gala performances. A few rather muddy cars were parked haphazardly in the street and a few people were standing in groups outside the building in animated conversation.

I went into the hall and came upon Miss Kiddle, sitting, very business-like, on a hassock on a kitchen chair, selling tickets behind a table. Her face lit up when she saw me.

"I thought you were going to miss seeing us," she cried. "But Fiona McLeod told me you were in town today and I hoped you'd come."

She took my ten pence piece and gave me half back in change, together with my ticket and a free programme, "with the compliments of the management."

"I've reserved a seat for you in the front row of the stalls on the right side," she said importantly. "The central one, next the aisle. You'll see everything from there."

I thanked her and passed on into the dreary auditorium and thought that really there had not been much need to reserve a seat, for the place was half empty. I could have had my choice of any one of the ten kitchen chairs, that formed the right half of the front row.

The front rows on the left were occupied by a contingent of children from the Lismore School, grouped under the fierce eye of the dominie. In front were ten small girls, all in tartan skirts and woollen jumpers, with silk ribbons to match the jumpers, tied in their fair curly hair. The row behind was full of boys, but their hair was subdued by being plastered to their skulls with cold water. In the third row, sat the dominie himself . . . a dreadful figure of stern discipline.

I sat down and glanced at the programme, which was type-written and had obviously passed through many hands, though nobody had thought fit to correct the three obvious errors in the subject matter. Of course, I had known what to expect. I edged round and studied the sprinkling of people behind me. There were about six Highland youths sitting together behind the dominie and they were almost certainly fans of Miss Barldrop, who was billed to appear in the curtain-raiser as the Spanish Lady, and then as Nerissa in extracts from the Merchant of Venice.

The hall was the prototype of all such places, with plaster flaking from the walls and a bare boarded floor, which had been scrubbed to a wonderful state of cleanliness. The house-lighting was supplied by bare electric bulbs, which hung suspended from the high ceiling on long flexes.

My chair was inclined to squeak every time I moved and to have become rather loose in its joints, so that it rocked a little from side to side. I shifted one seat along and finding that chair similarly affected, I finally came to rest on the third one in from the aisle. One of the youths left the group of Apryl's fans and came to sit beside me and from his demeanour, I thought it highly likely that he had been dared to do so by his companions, for he turned round and looked at them from time to time to nod and wink.

I studied the faded velvet curtains in front of me in an effort to ignore him, and almost at once, the overture commenced from somewhere behind the scenes, from a gramaphone record of Pomp and Circumstance, that had certainly seen better days.

Another five minutes and the curtains went back, but they stuck half way and were pulled hurriedly aside by hands, which appeared after a break of about five seconds. The young Scot at my side grunted to himself, as Apryl Barldrop was disclosed on stage, sitting left centre in the costume of a lady of Spain, with a high comb in her hair and a black lace mantilla draped down from it over her shoulders.

"I don't know why I am so sad today," she sighed and shot a glance at her friend beside me, and he shifted his raw-boned knees a bit and grinned at her.

It became abundantly obvious to me why she was so sad. Her father, played by Joshua Mardall in doublet and hose, with a ruff around his throat, was forcing her to wed a wealthy nobleman. Samuel Barldrop was cast as that gentleman and it was no wonder that Apryl was sad, for he was a most ruffianly looking grandee, and she was in love with Don Juan, played by Cedric, who at least had youth on his side.

It was a dreadful performance from start to finish. It had nothing to recommend it, unless you burlesqued it for the laughs, and then it might have brought down the house. They played it straight and the audience took it seriously and applauded loudly when Don Juan at last won the day. The cast took a few laborious curtains and I wondered why on earth somebody had not got the wretched tabs moving freely. It spoilt the whole effect and irritated me beyond measure, especially since Apryl thought that she could fill the heart of the young Scot at my side with jealousy, by ogling me in a revolting manner from behind her fan, as she took her bows.

I wondered what Miss Hemingway was doing and if she was nervous as she waited to come on and then Joshua Mardall came out in front, still in his Spanish costume and told us that we should now see extracts from William Shakespeare's immortal play the "Merchant of Venice." As the time was limited, and he made no mention of the cast being equally so, only the most important scenes would be played, and we must bear with him, if he described the action to fill in any gaps, that might arise. He told us about the first scene and then they went straight into the second, with Portia and her maid, Nerissa discovered on stage "in Belmont in a room in Portia's house." Apryl was still in her Spanish costume, but without the comb and mantilla.

I bent forwards with my elbows on my knees to watch Juliet Hemingway play Portia. Her voice was clear and pleasant and she certainly put every word across. She was as nervous as a cat for the first two minutes and then she settled down. She did not try to act Apryl off the stage. She was a good trouper. I got the impression that her acting had been influenced unduly by her school dramatic society, where it was just as likely they would have dressed her in breeches and made her a boy. I wondered what she would be like with expert direction and thought that she had possibilities. Then the great Mardall was on in the next scene, bent almost double, with his face hidden by a straggling beard and bushy brows, to play Shylock, the

Jew. He received a great ovation from the audience and he was not so bad as I had expected. If he had listened to my direction, I could have put him on in the Provinces and he would have got by with ease, if he had a good cast to support him. He was more than adequate in Lismore and they loved him.

He came out in front of the tabs, when the scene was over, apologized for not changing and got a laugh, before he described the further action of the play. Then Portia was on again with Bassanio in the Casket scene. Of course, Cedric was hopeless as a lover. Even my Ophelia could have made nothing of him, I thought. Juliet was Portia, but Cedric was Cedric . . . very conscious of his lady friends in the audience and given to winking at Juliet behind old Mardall's back throughout the production, with no thought of the action of the play.

I was happier about the trial scene. Mardall and Juliet were good together, or at any rate, they were adequate. She was clad in black doublet and hose by now, disguised as the "young and learned doctor" and she would have made an excellent Principal Boy in a Pantomime for her legs were long and shapely and she was beautifully proportioned and moved well.

I was bored by it all by that time and I committed the unpardonable sin of falling asleep, even with the discomfort of that chair. I was rather put out with her for not doing better with the lovely "Quality of Mercy" speech and I closed my eyes, but not for long. I dreamed that I was back in my flat and that Westlake had gone out to the hall to try to get rid of her. I heard her say in a cutting little voice:

"I see, sir, you are liberal in offers.

You taught me how to beg and now methinks
You teach me how a beggar should be answered . . . . "

I sat up in my seat with a jerk and heard Bassanio answer her and hoped that they had not noticed my lapse from grace, for it was infernal bad form on my part.

They finished the last scene eventually and took a few curtains and then old Mardall came out front and gave a flowery speech of appreciation for the way the show had been received. It was all rather pathetic. They seemed to be struggling against so many odds . . . bad props, inadequate lighting, poor costumes, hopeless stage. I thought of Miss Hemingway's appeal to appear in this type of production and smiled to myself. Bill, my dresser would have given notice for one thing, and I could imagine what Westlake would have made of the whole set-up. Yet Westlake had thought that I owed the girl an apology and there was no doubt that I did, not only for my behaviour in London, but for my supercilious remarks about the Company, when I had met her in Lismore. I wondered how one asked for an interview in the star's dressing-room, for now was the time to get it done and finished with. I decided to seek out my friend Hermione Kiddle and as I thought about her, she appeared like a fairy gnome at my side, I stood up to greet her, but she wriggled herself onto the seat at my side, which the young man had vacated, where she sat with her legs dangling.

"Sit down!" she commanded briskly. "You're too far away up there."

I sat down beside her and turned to look down at her square cheerful face. God knows she had very little to be so cheerful about.

"How did you like our performance?" she asked me

and I told her that I had enjoyed it very much.

She was suddenly serious.

"It's not what it used to be. I should like you to have seen us ten years ago, when we had the full company. Mr. Mardall was famous all over the country for his interpretation of Othello."

I took out my note-case and saw her eyes glance for a moment at the magnificence of its gold-bound crocodile. It would not matter, I thought, for I should tell Miss Hemingway who I was and make my apology.

"I would very much like to go round and see Miss Hemingway," I said. "I want to congratulate her and I owe her an apology, which must be made in person."

I opened the case and took out a card, but Miss Kiddle got off her chair with a sideways shuffle and shook her head at me.

"A card, Mr. John?" she smiled. "Surely not? And that wallet isn't right for the costume either. We shall never make an actor out of you. You're bad at disguises."

"But . . . " I began and she went off along the row of chairs with a laugh.

"No need to be so formal. Just come along with me and I'll bring you to her dressing room. She'll be delighted that you enjoyed the show and it will do her good to get some praise from such a personable young man, for she's got too poor an opinion of herself by half."

She conducted me through a door at the side of the stage and down a long corridor. She asked me to wait for a moment while she went into one of the rooms and presently, she was back again.

"She'll see you at once, Mr. John and I've changed my opinion about that beard of yours, not that it's grown a bit. Don't have it off at any price."

She grinned all over her pleasant face.

"And don't produce that note case nor yet the cigarette lighter, if you want to act the part, you've picked out for yourself to play, which doesn't suit you one bit. You're tailor-made for elegance and gracious living. Don't tell me you're not!"

She went off along the corridor in her brisk waddling way and I went into the large square room, that was evidently the ladies' dressing room.

It had a wainscotting of wood varnished to look like grained oak, and above this, the walls were scaling green plaster. A single light bulb without a shade hung down from the ceiling on a rather fuzzy flex and somebody had led off another wire to provide a powerful bulb over a kitchen table against one wall. Juliet was sitting at this table with her make-up kit littered in front of her and Apryl was changing her costume behind a moth-eaten screen in the corner. I crossed over and sat on the edge of the table and looked down at Juliet's face under the glare of the light. The harshness of the setting could not detract from her beauty. She had wiped off her paint and her face was shining with cold cream, but she was even lovelier than I had remembered her from her first close-up in my arms. Her dark lashes fanned dark shadows on the perfect planes of her cheeks, as she looked down at the table.

"Did the Strolling Players please your Majesty?"

She was pretending to joke, but she was mighty serious about it.

"Very well indeed," I told her and saw the iridescence, the light made on the crown of her dark head. "I came behind to congratulate you on a very excellent portrayal of Portia."

She picked up the colour pencil and made up her mouth and her eyes came to meet mine in the mirror.

"You were right, weren't you?" she said and held out a fold of her gown for me to see. "Moth-eaten, just as you said."

I felt very awkward with her.

"I want to apologize about that. It was an unforgivable thing for me to say and I didn't mean it. Besides, costumes matter very little. It's the players inside them, who are important."

"Did you think Cedric was good?" she asked me in a direct way, which was like as if she held a pistol at my head.

"Of course," I said, but my voice lacked conviction.

"And Apryl?"

Apryl came out from behind her screen, stretching her arms above her head and yawning. She had changed to her ballet tights, but above the waist, she wore nothing but a black brassiere. She was giving a show, which she considered suitable for the average stage-door johnny and she came langurously over to admire herself in the glass. She sighed and looked at me sideways out of heavily mascaraed eyes.

"Was I good?" she asked and I resisted an impulse to tell her to go away and stop wasting her time and mine.

"You were adequate," I said gravely.

"Adequate, the man says." she said dreamily and drifted sinuously off towards the door, picking up her sweater on the way.

"And Joshua?" Juliet said abruptly. "Was Joshua a good Shylock?"

I looked down at the toe of my shoe, which I was swinging too and fro.

"Is this a catechism?" I smiled. "Of course, he was very good indeed."

I glanced back at her face and was horrified to see that she was not far from tears. The door shut with a slam, as Apryl went out, and Juliet dabbed the powder puff into the round box of powder and patted it on her face.

"Oh, God!" she said. "The people here will soon see the great Olivier or Schofield or Jonathan Harley himself, playing Hamlet . . . and Shylock . . . and Othello . . . and Lear . . . on television screens in every parish hall in Scotland, and what then?"

She put a hand out and laid it on my knee and looked up into my face earnestly.

"Was Joshua good? Was he?"

"He was fine," I said and watched the tears gathering in her eyes.

"Yet you went asleep," she accused me. "Right in the middle of his most dramatic scene, you went asleep."

"I was tired. The fault was mine . . . not yours. I haven't been too well."

"You're a liar," she said in a small dreary voice and put up a hand to dash the tears from her eyes. Her sleeve caught on a splinter of wood and tore in a great triangular rent and she looked down at it in despair.

"It's rotten," she whispered. "It's no good. I don't know what to do about it . . . there's nothing to do. I'm no good either, am I?"

I took my handkerchief out of my pocket and leaned down to wipe away the slow tears, that trickled down her cheeks like drops of crystal, feeling the old miserable heaviness in my chest.

"Don't weep about it," I said. "It'll be all right. You'll see."

"You're kind," she said. "You tell kind lies. It will never be all right. I thought I could pull it together, but I can't."

"I think that perhaps I might be able to help you."

I was surprised to hear my voice as husky with emotion, as ever it had been on any stage. She smiled through her tears.

"And what could your Majesty do?"

"I don't know. I'll think of something."

"Don't get involved with us," she begged me. "We're finished and on the way out. Hermione Kiddle says that you're in some trouble as it is. Don't get dragged further down with us."

I slid off the table and put a hand on her downcast head.

"Perhaps I'll think of something to get the Strolling Players right up on top . . . make them famous from Land's End to John O' Groats?"

I laughed to try to rally her from her dismal mood, but she put her head down on the table and asked me not to joke about it.

This was the moment to tell her who I was. I caught her by the shoulders and spun her round and lifted her up to stand in front of me and marvelled at the slenderness of her between my hands.

"I . . . " I began and then "I . . . " again, and could not find the words to tell her I was the great Jonathan Harley, because of the effect she was having on my senses. If she had been a woman of fire, she could not have had a greater effect on me. There was a burning tingling sensation that ran up my arms and pervaded my whole body and turned my insides to water.

"You've got no faith in me," I said after a while. "Don't you think I could help you?"

"Nobody could do anything to help us," she said. "Not in a thousand years. It's very kind of you, but . . . . "

I looked at her luminous blue eyes and saw the small specks of black in the irises. I saw the long lashes damp with her tears, and her soft red mouth. I knew if I stayed in the room any longer, that no power on earth could stop me raising her into my arms, to hold her close to my breast and kiss her, so I let her go and she sat down limply on her chair.

"Perhaps you're right," I said. "We'll see."

I went off across the floor and through the door and down the corridor and jumped down the front steps, and surprised Apryl in the front seat of the Land Rover in Jamie Stewart's arms. He sprang away from her, as if he had been stung, when he saw me and grinned at me sheepishly.

"I was bidin' till ye cam'," he said. "We'll awa' hame noo."

I climbed into the car and we said goodnight to Apryl and Jamie promised to drive over to see the show at Laragh the next week. A thick fog had come down and we made our way out slowly and perilously along the cliff road, while I wondered what Juliet would have done if I had kissed her. I had never felt so attracted to any woman before, either on or off stage and I marvelled at it. Jamie was also meditating on the state of his heart, for he paid far too little attention to his driving and nearly had us over the cliff once or twice. Now and again, he sighed deeply.

"Yon lassie," he said once. "I doot she'd mak' a guid wifie for a farmer."

I told him that perhaps she could adapt herself. After all, she was very young and if she loved a man, she would try to fall in with his ways.

"I doot she's in love wi' anybody but hersel'," he said mournfully.

There was silence between us, while we thought of Apryl Barldrop adjusting herself to a Highland farm.

"I canna see her milkin' the coos in yon trews," he said, at last.

"Oh, I don't know about that," I remarked falsely. I thanked him when he stopped at the white gate to let me down, but I do not think he heard me. His mind was still fully occupied with thoughts of Miss Barldrop.

"Och, ma mither wid kill me," he sighed. "She's o' the opinion that Apryl's triflin' wi' ma affections, and I wid na be surprised if she was na right. She's a tarrible flirt."

The fog closed behind the Land Rover, as he drove off and I walked along the grassy track to the cottage, feeling my way through the invisibility and hoping that I would not end up by falling over into the sea. I could not have felt more at peace with the world, if I had been strolling through summer meadows, with the lark's song high in the sky above me. The hazel grove was dripping and silent and eerie in the grey blackness and the murmur of the waves sounded a long way off. I was glad when I got to the cottage and creaked the door open. I snapped on my lighter and set the flame to the candles and then I heaped dry wood onto the ashes in the grate. I changed into my pyjamas and dressing gown and sat full length in the arm chair with a glass of Old Mull in my hand and began to try to figure out some way of helping the Strolling Players. There was a cold logical section of my brain that told me that I was a fool to get mixed up with them at all. It might be a difficult business, one way and another. There was no need for me to come out into the open and tell Juliet who I was . . . no need to apologize for that matter. It had been a ridiculous idea for her to expect me to appear in a show of that class. The wise thing, my common sense told me, would be to send them a generous donation. That was the practical way out of the whole situation. Bert Hollidge . . . the stage manager and presumably, Ann Perry too, who had also come to my flat that day, had been content with my help. Yet, that way, I would never see her again and there was no doubt in my mind that I must see her again. I pushed the thought of her out of my brain and climbed into bed with the script of Bothwell in my hand, but Juliet kept getting mixed up with Mary, Queen of Scots in a fantastic manner. She glided into all my thoughts, dressed in Tudor costume, with the high Medici collar about her white throat and the coif graceful above the peak of raven hair on her forehead. I threw the book on the floor at last and blew out the candle and then she entrenched herself firmly in my imagination. I held her shoulders between my hands and felt the slenderness of her again, saw the dark lashes fanned on the smooth perfection of her cheeks. I bent my head and laid my mouth on hers and knew well that I must see her again, and see her again very soon. With Jamie, I thought, I would go over to Laragh and see the show. I wondered where Laragh was, and if I could persuade Jamie to give me a lift in the Land Rover, or if his "Mither" would kill us both, if she found out where we were going. I smiled to myself and was asleep, and the next moment or so it seemed, I was awakened by the sound of crashing metal and breaking glass. I tried to wake up. For a second, I thought it had been a dream and then I heard somebody shout. My lighter went flying onto the floor, when I groped for it and it was a long time before I found it again and lit the candle. I grabbed my dressing-gown off the end of the bed and pushed my feet into slippers and ran to open the door. The fog swirled in all around me and I could hear a man's voice shouting in the direction of the cliff edge.

"Who's there?" I called.

There was a glare of diffused light near the hazel grove and I walked carefully towards it and bumped up against the side of the old yellow bus, which belonged to the Players. I groped my way along towards the bonnet and found Miss Kiddle standing by her Austin, her small hands clasped in front of her in dismay. The lights from the bus illuminated the scene for ten feet, perhaps, but no more.

"The gate wasn't shut," she cried. when she saw who it was. "Joshua's car gone over the cliff. We saw we'd come wrong and Juliet was trying to turn it round."

I bent down and seized her by the shoulders, full of a dreadful feeling of fear and foreboding.

"Has she gone over the cliff?" I asked her.

"It's all right, Joshua pulled her out, when the back wheels began to slide. She got a fright, but she's safe enough. It's only the car."

I ran away from her towards where I thought the cliff should be, but I blundered into the grove and got caught up with brambles and fell down over a tree stump. I made a nice mess of myself one way and another, with thorns and mud and wet branches. It must have been five minutes, before I came suddenly upon Joshua Mardall with his arm round Juliet, staring down into the sea. As it was, I almost went over the cliff myself with my foolish running about, because the fog was very thick indeed by now and the shouting seemed to come from every direction at once.

"Is anybody hurt?" I gasped out at Joshua and he switched his torch up into my face to see who I was and succeeded in blinding me totally for a moment or two.

"Only poor William," he said sorrowfully. "He'll be smashed to pieces on the rocks down there . . . the poor old fellow. I've had him for fifty years . . . fifty years."

I turned round and ran towards the cliff steps.

"I'll go down and see . . . " I shouted back over my shoulder, and was horrified to see flames glowing pinkly far below me.

"It's no good going down there," said Sam Barldrop, appearing out of the fog at my side. "There's nothing to be done and you'll break your neck. We'll see to it in the morning."

"But William . . . " I began and he gave a dour grunt.

"It's only the bust of William Shakespeare. It was in the back of the Hillman, but it's well insured, like everything else. At least Joshua was no fool about insurance."

I went back and found Juliet and took her hand in mine and then we rounded up Miss Kiddle and Apryl. In five minutes we were all back inside the cottage and the fire was beginning to burn up the dry wood I had thrown on it. Meggie Barldrop was the motherly one of the troupe. We established the others in front of the the fire and she and I went into the kitchen to forage for food. In no time at all, we had the black kettle singing over the flames in the open hearth, while Juliet and Apryl were set to toast muffins. Sam went off to the bus and came back with sausages and Meggie fried them in a pan over the Beatrice stove. Soon we were sitting having an excellent picnic meal in front of a blazing fire and feeling our spirits lift appreciably.

Joshua Mardall sat back in the arm chair at last and took out an enamelled snuff box out of his vest pocket. He held it out towards me.

"Do you partake, sir?"

I shook my head and he took a pinch of snuff himself in a most graceful manner. Then he brushed his nostrils with an elegant spotted silk handkerchief. He gazed sadly into the fire.

"An act of the Almighty," he sighed. "As all misfortunes are."

I got up and stood with one arm on the mantlepiece and looked down at him.

"I'm most awfully sorry, sir. It was completely my fault. I forgot to close the gate and there's no excuse for my carelessness. I suppose it was the bad weather, but I'm responsible for any damage done and of course, I'll settle up for it."

His eye went round the cottage for a moment and he shook his head.

"Of course not, my boy. Don't you put yourself out about it. Any person might have omitted to close the gate on such a night and anyhow we had no right to drive into your property, gate or no gate."

"But you don't know . . . " I started.

"The poor visibility was completely to blame," he declared. "You have been kind enough to offer us the hospitality of your home. Tir-nan-oge . . . a lovely name for an enchanted place. We're honoured to be your guests."

"But there's something I'd better tell you now," I said and in my agitation I knocked the miniature of Jonathan flying onto the ground at his feet. He picked it up and looked at it.

"I see you're an admirer of the great Harley," he remarked, gazing down at it. "A fine man, Harley! A prince of the theatre! Full of the humanities too."

"As a matter of fact . . . " I began and then thought what a strange looking sight I must appear to them in my muddy dressing gown with my hiar tousled all about my head.

"Did you read that speech he made recently?" he asked. "It was widely reported in the Press, and quite rightly so."

I sat down on the floor and leaned up against the chair he had just vacated, so that I could be near Juliet, and Joshua Mardall made a theatrical gesture and delivered the quotation in his flowery style.

"ANY GOOD THING THEREFORE THAT I CAN DO OR ANY KIND-NESS THAT I CAN SHOW TO ANY FELLOW CREATURE, LET ME DO IT NOW. LET ME NOT DEFER IT OR NEGLECT IT, FOR I SHALL NOT PASS THIS WAY AGAIN."

I looked sideways at Juliet and she was frowning a little.

"It's simple enough to say a thing like that," she said with a sharp edge to her voice. "If to do were as easy as to know what to do, chapels had been churches . . . . " She was quoting the "Merchant" again, but the others were onto her in a flash. Apparently Jonathan Harley was a general favourite.

"Come now, Juliet!" cried old Mardall. "That's a foolish thing for you to say."

"What's got into you anyway?" demanded Meggie Barldrop. "I thought you always had a great passion for him."

"Jealous of his leading ladies, that's what's up with her," said Cedric.

Juliet's nose rose an inch into the air.

"I used to like him, when I was young," she said primly. "I don't like him now. He's proud and he's conceited and he has no interest in anything but the mighty Jonathan Harley. He acts everybody else off the stage and he's unfaithful, as well as everything else."

"Unfiathful —" echoed Meggie. "He's not even married.'

Her daughter, Apryl looked at her pityingly.

"You don't have to be married to be unfaithful," she scoffed. "He has lovers . . . hundreds of them."

Samuel Barldrop got up and shuffled off into the kitchen with a frown at Meggie.

"You oughtn't to allow your daughter to say such things," he said. "I don't know what the world's coming to, when young girls discuss the like of that."

Apryl paid him not the slightest heed.

"His latest woman is Sally Druce. Blond she is . . . platinum . . . but it's natural. She played Ophelia at the Festival in Edinburgh and she's gorgeous. He's head over heels in love with her, but he's not the marrying kind. I could tell her a thing or two about him. His whole life has been paved with broken hearts."

"He won't break my heart," said Juliet.

"Don't you wish he had the chance to try?" laughed Cedric and she looked at him scornfully.

"He doesn't attract me in the slightest," she said. "Of course, he's not bad on the stage, but I think he's overrated."

I put a hand on her shoulder gently.

"Have you ever seen him on the stage?" I asked her and she shook her head and said that she had only seen Harley at the cinema.

I pinned her down.

"Are you sure that he leads an immoral life?" I asked her and she hedged a bit, but Miss Barldrop went in heavily on her side.

"He's like an alley-cat," she said. "He's as bad as Don Juan, Henry the Eighth and Robbie Burns put together."

I looked at her and felt a strong desire to warm the seat of her black trews and then turn my attention to my lady, Juliet.

"I thought he was a very good-living chap," I said. "It just shows you. I don't think I'll have such a high opinion of him in the future."

I could see that Juliet was having qualms of conscience about bearing false witness.

"I don't really know if he has many lady friends," she said in a troubled voice. "It's probably only gossip, but I do know that he's very conceited and I do know that he doesn't practice what he preaches."

"I bet you he's not a virgin all the same," laughed Apryl. "Not with eyes like he's got. Bedroom eyes, that's what they are. He sort of undresses you, when he looks at you."

Her father came back into the room in a towering rage.

"If you don't get those girls off to bed this minute," he told Meggie. "I'll lay them across my knee and skelp them. I don't know what the world is coming to, when the Company indulges in such discussion in public."

I smiled up at the Punch and Judy man and thought what a wise-looking old fellow he was. He shook his head sorrowfully.

"Jonathan Harley is a fine man," he said. "Don't listen to all the curs, that yap at his heels."

Cedric got to his feet and did a little tap dance on the floor.

"Old Ape would like to break down his resistance, if he is a virgin," he laughed, and his sister jumped sideways at him in a flying tackle, that brought him to the ground with a bump. Old Barldrop looked down at his two children engaged in an all-in wrestling bout on the floor and he sniffed dourly.

"I don't know how we bred them, Meggie," he said. "They must take after your brother, Jo, that was on the high wire, because they're not like you, nor yet me. I just don't know."

I was glad when the combat had been resolved and the discussion turned to the topic of where we were all going to sleep for the rest of the night. We settled the ladies down in the cottage eventually and went off to the bus, but I could not go to sleep. The thoughts were whizz-banging in my brain like jumping crackers. There was no doubt that I must make some effort to help them now. Yet, what could I do with a Punch and Judy show and a fortune-teller, and a trio of green juveniles with no idea of discipline, led by a barnstorming old patriarch like Father Noah? I got up at last and went quietly out of the bus and saw that the fog had cleared away and that the morning was coming up bright and fair and I shivered in the cold breeze, that was coming in off the sea. I sat down on a rock near the cliff edge and I expect I gave a tolerable picture of misery to Old Joshua, as he came slowly along the grass to talk to me. He draped a blanket over my shoulders and sat down to put a fatherly hand on my arm. "Nothing is as bad as that, my boy," he said. "Don't think that I haven't known the depths of despair too, but you've got youth on your side. Never admit defeat. Never strike the flag. Tomorrow is another day."

I thought sarcastically of adding "And every cloud has a silver lining," but wisely held my tongue, and he sat looking out to sea for a long time, before he spoke again, in a very sad voice.

"I'd like to be able to help you, but it's almost beyond my powers, as matters stand. You can join the company, if you like, for you shouldn't be left alone here, without a friend to talk to. It's strange how I picked them all up the same way . . . the ones, who stuck to me, when the others deserted the sinking ship."

I do not think that he had any consciousness of my presence as he went on.

"I had a full company of twenty first-rate players, playing the big provincial towns too, when I met old Sam . . . poor old Punch and Judy, pawning his coat to buy food. Cedric was a little curly headed boy and Apryl was a babe in arms . . . and Hermione Kiddle, there's a kind heart for you . . . worth a hundred of the dolts, who laughed at her. You could put your life in her hands . . . . And Juliet too, more like her mother every day. Regina, I called my daughter. That's Juliet's name too. Juliet Regina Hemingway . . . a little schoolgirl in a navy gaberdine coat and two long black plaits to her waist. Ten she was the day of the funeral and her eyes red from the tears, she'd shed, and no wonder. Both in one grave, my Regina and her bonnie laddie . . . in one grave."

He sighed deeply and then came out of his reverie suddenly and looked at me.

"There's an end to everything. This will be my last season, for there's no escaping it now."

He took my shoulder in his hand.

"You're not to worry about that infernal gate. It wasn't done on purpose and I can see that you're in no position to pay damages. I presume you make your living making those walking sticks . . . ."

I did not know what he meant for a moment, and then I saw that he meant my rams' horn ash sticks. He must have noticed them in the cottage. I thought that the farce had gone on long enough. It was high time that I told him who I was and that I could afford to pay a hundred times over for his whole miserable show. I stood up and wrapped the blanket round me like an Indian brave.

"Look here, sir. I think I had better tell you that I'm not what I seem to be . . . ."

"It's quite obvious, my boy," he smiled. "You'd never make an actor, you know. You talk braw Scots to Fiona McLeod, but when you meet Sam, you're speaking like an Oxford Don. You grow a beard to hide your face and you live out in this remote place. Your clothes are torn and shabby, but they're like you . . . they've seen better days. You've got an expensive gold cigarette lighter and a very fine wrist watch. You need only tell me one thing and I'd be glad of an honest answer to that, for I've got the ladies under my protection."

He looked at me intently.

"Have you done anything dishonourable?"

"It was nothing dishonourable," I assured him.

"But you are in hiding. We're right about that?"

I thought of Sally Druce and wished Westlake could hear the conversation.

"I suppose that you could put it like that."

His hand came down on my shoulder.

"Well, young man, if it's any help to you, you're welcome to join the Company. You'll never make an actor, but you can do your best. At least you'll have a month or two. You may have found your salvation by then, and you'll have companionship."

He looked at the morning beauty of the mountains across the sea.

"A man could go insane living close to trouble in a place like this. It'll be better when you've got friends about you. You'll see. It always is."

He partook of a pinch of snuff in his grand manner and brushed his nose with the spotted silk handkerchief, and I felt very touched by his kindness to me, yet I wondered if I should tell him who I was and not get entangled with any more deception. I thanked him sincerely and did not decline nor accept, but went across to the cottage to fetch my towel and my bathing trunks and then I made my way down the cliff steps for my morning swim. There was nothing to be seen of the yellow Hillman, but a few tangled sheets of scorched metal, for the tide had come in and washed over the wreckage. I went to the flat rock and was irritated when Cedric joined me, wearing an atrocious pair of scarlet satin trunks, that did nothing to flatter his bony frame. He did a step dance on the rock and ended it up with a side-ways spring like a ballet dancer, in which he clapped his two feet together, before he touched the ground again.

"In sooth!" he grinned. "Thou hast the body of a Greek God, thou lucky so-and-so. If I be not wrong, thou makest the maidens to lie down and roll in the aisles."

I grunted sourly and dived into the brilliant clear water to get rid of him, but he was in after me in a flash in a flat ungraceful dive, and he dogged me in a manner, which quite infuriated me, swimming round in breast stroke with no style in the world but his own.

He spouted a mouthful of water up in the air and grinned again.

"Thou swimmest like a Greek God also," he shouted. "Wait until my sister, the lady Apryl clappeth eyes upon you in your bathing attire. She will desire your scalp above all things, to hang about her slender girdle."

I looked at him rather coldly and turned and did a slow crawl for about two hundred yards out to sea. He called after me as I went.

"Don't go too far out there, old chap. There's a hell of a current."

I pretended not to hear him, for he annoyed me beyond endurance. I floated about for ten minutes or so and then I noticed that I had drifted north along the coast a little way. I rolled over and started to make my way back towards the flat rock and I was surprised when I made no headway. In another five minutes, I was alarmed. There was no doubt that I had been a fool not to have heeded Cedric's warning. I saw that he had noticed my predicament, for he had scrambled out of the sea and was clambering along the rocks, trying to keep level with my drift. His mouth opened and shut as he shouted encouragement, which of course, I could not hear.

I put on a tremendous spurt and was frightened, when I saw I was being taken further out than ever. I knew that there was a small cove about two miles along the coast . . . a kind of estuary, and I wondered if I would come in there. If I was lucky, there might be a dinghy anchored there and Cedric could row out and pick me ingloriously out of the sea.

I came round the headland of the cove in a swirling bubbling wash, that seemed to be sweeping into the inlet with the flowing tide. It was a nasty race of water, full of eddies and little whirling currents, and it took me under three or four times and made me feel more alarmed than ever. I was getting very fagged and short of breath and I had had a few mouthfuls of sea water, that did nothing to improve my courage. Still, I thought I had a good chance of making it, although there was no dinghy in sight. I put on a final spurt and felt cramp doubling me like a jack knife. I went under for what seemed an age and breathed in salt water again and then I surfaced for ten seconds and went down, knowing that this was the end of Jonathan Harley. A handful of sparks exploded inside my head and I began a desperate struggle for air, knowing that it was hopeless.

I came up out of the blackness to see a pair of legs covered with blood. They were thin bony shanks with fair hair all matted in the blood and they meant nothing to me. I could not remember what had happened.

"Don't worry, Juliet. He's almost round. He's not going to die yet."

That was Meggie Barldrop's voice, I thought and wondered who Meggie Barldrop was. Then I saw that the legs belonged to Cedric. They were gashed horribly at the knees and down the shins. He limped away to sit at a rock pool and his mother bent to bathe his wounds with her handkerchief.

"Och, Mum, go easy with that salt water. It stings like hell."

Somebody was wiping my face gently and I looked up and saw Juliet's eyes, as she stooped over me. Her dark hair was swinging about her face and her brow was wrinkled.

"You'll feel better in a minute, Mr. John. Cedric pulled you out just in time, but he got cut on the barnacles. One of your knees is cut too, but it's nothing. I've done it up for you."

I shook my head and tried to sit up, and felt her arm come round me. I leaned my head on her shoulder and she stroked my hair off my forehead with her hand.

"Meggie and I saw you from the cliff. You shouldn't have gone out so far. We ran along the path, but Cedric had got you out, when we got here. He's by way of being a hero."

I leaned forward and put my head in my hands. I felt physically sick, but far worse, I felt sick with myself, when I thought that this boy, whom I had despised, had saved my life and had hurt himself doing it too. Worse than that, Joshua Mardall had offered me a job, because he thought I was down and out. It was the same kind of gesture that Hermione Kiddle had made, when she shared her sandwiches with me. Yet, I had felt myself a superior being to them all . . . I, the great Harley . . . idol of millions. I sat there and saw myself for what I was . . . an egocentric, conceited popinjay, of no more importance than Sam Barldrop's Mr. Punch, and with about the same social conscience as that gentleman.

"Any man's death diminishes me, because I am involved in mankind. And therefore never send to know for whom the bell tolls. It tolls for thee," I mumbled.

Juliet's lips tickled my ear.

"It's all right," she whispered and her dark hair brushed my face. "You're not going to die, and we'll have you home and into your bed in a jiffy. Hermione is to bring the car down by the road. You'll only have to walk a hundred yards. You can lean your weight on me."

I sat up and looked across at Cedric.

"You saved my life," I said.

He only grinned at me.

"Think nothing of it, Sir Knight," he laughed. "I would have got into great trouble with the lady Apryl, my sister, if I had let thee drown that gorgeous body of thine."

He tried to do his usual little step dance on the rock and pulled a rueful face.

"You saved my life," I repeated. "Your legs are horribly cut. You must be in great pain. Oh, God! I don't know how one thanks a person, who gives back one's whole future."

He winked at me and then winced again, as Meggie began to bind up his legs with strips torn from her petticoat.

"Thou can'st decide to be a most valorous knight in ye future," he said. "Get thee hence and marry the maiden."

I did not find his humour atrocious any more. One is not critical of the person who has just saved one's life.

"There's no maiden," I smiled at him and wondered if this was the time to tell them who I was. At least Mistress Juliet would feel mighty awkward about her allegations against Jonathan Harley's character last night. I leaned back against her shoulder once more and felt the softness of her slender body and the fragrance of her hair.

"My name isn't John or Mr. John," I sighed. "I'd better begin at the beginning and tell you the whole story, but I doubt if you'll believe me."

Juliet put her cheek against mine. "We all know it's not. There's no need to tell us anything about it. Joshua has told us that you're one of the Company now and we're all very pleased to have you. We won't pry into your past."

They were all agreed on that. They stood round smiling down at me and nodding their heads.

"It's your business . . . not ours," Meggie said. "We're all friends here. One for all and all for one, and each person trying to think of the other chap, as well as himself."

I saw that there was a pattern to the whole thing. It would be easy enough to say that I was Jonathan Harley now . . . to see the wonder come into their eyes . . . to have their praise and adulation . . . to pour out money on their show and bolster it up with a few picked troupers, but it could not be done like that. There was penance to be done . . . ashes to be put on the head, and pride to be humbled.

"You won't be able to drive the bus," I said to Cedric. "I can manage that, if you show me how. I can drive a car."

He grinned at me.

"You'll have to fill in on the stage for me too. I'm not going to be able to wear hose for a few weeks, but don't look so frightened. You'll get used to it and Joshua can put on bits, where I don't come in much. Acting is as easy as falling off a log. You just pick out a pretty girl in the front row of the stalls and give her the eye. It all comes automatically then and you forget you're on."

So that was what was wrong with Master Cedric's acting, I thought.

"I'll bear it in mind," I told him gravely.

"You'll have to have that beard off," he said, and Juliet tightened her arm about my shoulder.

"Of course, he won't have to have his beard off," she said. "Why do you think he grew it in the first place? We all know that part of it and besides, it looks most distinguished."

She stood up and began to help me to my feet.

"We must try to get home. The sooner we get you into bed, the better it'll be and don't even think about the acting. I'll show you how to do it. I'll help you learn your parts and everything else. We'll get along splendidly. You'll be just as good as Cedric in no time at all. You'll see. We'll get along splendidly!"

I sat in the cottage the next afternoon and pretended to learn my lines for Bassanio. I had made an almost complete recovery from my near-drowning, but I had insisted on Cedric being kept in bed. His legs were in a dreadful way and Miss Kiddle had run him in to the doctor's to have them dressed and to fetch some ointment and bandages for future use. We had postponed our appearance at Laragh for a week, during which time, we hoped to be able to get some semblance of order into the production. We had camped out quite comfortably in the cottage and Tir-nan-oge had changed from being a solitary place, to a centre of bustling activity and good fellowship. I found that I was happier than I had ever been in my life before, and knew it was because I had Juliet at my side the livelong day.

We had a magnificent tea that afternoon and I ate far too many potato cakes, dripping with butter. Apryl picked up my tea cup, when I put it down empty at last and looked over at Meggie.

"Tell his fortune, Mum."

Sam Barldrop frowned at her.

"Mr. John's too smart a man to believe in fortunes and tea cups and all that twaddle."

Meggie inverted my cup on the saucer and turned it round three times, before she glanced at me enquiringly.

"If you tell fortunes as well as you make potato cakes, I shan't grumble."

She took the cup between her two hands and peered into it with great interest, as she tried to compose her dumpling of a face into the mysterious expression of a seer into the mists of the future.

"That's funny," she said at last and picked up my hand to gaze earnestly into the palm. She had put the cup on the table and she sat down beside me and lifted her brown eyes to my face.

"You're not what you seem to be," she said, with her brow wrinkled. "It's in the cup and again in your hand. It's not what I thought . . . . "

"Oh, shut up, Mum." cried Apryl inelegantly and put her hand up to feel my bearded jaw. "That's cheating. We all know that. Tell us about his love life."

"Do you want your ears boxed, Madam?" asked Sam,

but Meggie was staring into my palm and her voice was puzzled.

"You're a man of outstanding talent . . . way . . . way above normal. There's wealth and fame all about you. You'll go to the top of the tree."

She glanced at my face suddenly and back to my palm. "Perhaps you've been there and had a fall. I can't see that part clearly, but you're a man of good character . . . a fine man with ideals."

Juliet sat down at my feet and leaned her back against my legs.

"Indeed, your Majesty will get too full of stinking pride," she laughed. "Can't you see anything bad, Meggie?"

"Balderdash!" cried old Sam. "Don't you believe a word of it. You women should think shame of yourselves."

"It's funny," went on Meggie in a dreamy way. "It's the same story in the cup and the hand. Give me the cards, Apryl. Let's see if they tell the same thing."

She put the greasy thickened pack of cards into my hand and told me to shuffle them and cut them out upon the table in packs of three. Apryl pushed back the tea things and we all went over to the table, while I dealt out the cards with great solemnity. Meggie picked up one pile of them and began to place them down very deliberately in a strange arrangement rather like a pentagon. Then she spread the rest of them around that, taking great care to put them in a certain pattern. She looked at them for a long time, and then she turned to me.

"It's the same here. I've never seen anything like it. It's written in the cards . . . strongly . . . very, very strongly. There's no doubt about it."

She tapped the King of Spades.

"Here you are. That's your card. Look how the Queens are all about you. The Queen of Hearts, the Queen of Spades, the Queen of Clubs, the Queen of Diamonds. All beautiful women gathered about you. Look at them . . . talented women, rich women, beautiful women and you can take your pick of them for they've all got hearts for you . . . See how they crowd about you."

Apryl giggled a little and came over to lean on the back of my chair in a confidential way, breathing heavily down the back of my neck.

"Gee!" she exclaimed. "I never saw anything like it. Which is his true love, Mum?"

Meggie had picked up the cards and was shuffling them and dealing them out again in a small pile. She threw the Queen of Spades down on the table under my nose.

"There's your lady," she said triumphantly. "As dark as you are yourself . . . lovely, accomplished, kind."

"Poppycock, poppycock and more poppycock!" Sam Barldrop exploded. "It's flying in the face of the Almighty. That's what it is."

Joshua took a pinch of snuff and went to stand with his back to the fire.

"I wouldn't say that, Samuel," he pronounced in his grand way, and then brushed his nose with the spotted silk handkerchief. "It keeps the ladies out of mischief and it's far better than the other night, when they were taking a man's character away, with just as little thought as they're giving now to telling a man's future life."

Meggie ignored them completely, as did we all, come to that. We were all around the table by this time and Meggie was spinning out my fortune in the way of such things.

"The Queen of Spades has hearts for you. Look at that."

She dealt out three heart cards in quick succession.

"And here's your card for her. See what it is. The Ace of hearts. You love her as much as it is possible for a man to love his lady . . . and money now, watch out for the diamonds . . . not many of those at first. She's not a wealthy woman, but she's got talent. There's money to come to her and not from you . . . money from her own talent. Here she is again, with beauty and gentleness and loving you as you love her, but there's a barrier between you."

There was no doubt that Meggie believed all she told me. Her brow was wrinkled and her voice worried.

"I can't see what this thing is between you and your true love. There are people round and lights and a journey, with you far apart. You're trying to get back to her and you're blocked at every turn of the cards . . . here and here and here again. You're going on a journey . . . . "

"I reckon he's going to try another trip out to sea," laughed Cedric. "That's the barrier reef you see."

Meggie did not seem to hear him. She looked at me and her eyes were serious and sad.

"I can't see the way back. Maybe, there's no way back. Maybe you'll never meet your Queen of Spades again. There are tears all about her and unhappiness for you and doubts between you both, and both of your hearts broken. I can't see the end of it. Perhaps it's happiness, but if it is, I can't see it in the cards."

"I never met such a woman for upsetting herself over nothing," exclaimed her husband, taking the cards from her and putting them firmly in the cupboard. One of these days, I'll burn those blasted cards. You see if I don't."

Old Mardall smiled benignly.

"Besides which, it's time Bassanio was learning his part. There are very few days left before his stage debut and he is in no way practised at memorising great tracts of blank verse. Take him into the open air, Juliet. Help him all you can. We'll appoint you his instructress in chief, and we'll hold you responsible if he folds up on the first night."

Juliet and I took a rug out and sat in the glory of the red sunset and I had an idyllic hour or two with her in the still of the evening, with only the gulls' cry in our ears and the music of the waterfall. I looked my fill at her earnest face, seeing her luminous, clear eyes and the loveliness of her mouth. The light wind lifted the hair from her forehead and I wanted to put out a hand and feel the silkiness of its texture. We sat down on the rug and her eyes were dreaming, as she looked out towards the mountains over the sea.

"It's like Tir-nan-oge over there," she said. "The land of the ever-young."

"That name's from Irish legend, isn't it?" I asked her. "Do you know the story?"

She clasped her hands round her knees and sat forward.

"Tir-nan-oge is a land inhabited by the little people . . . the fairies," she told me. "But mortals are sometimes brought there and are given the gift of eternal youth."

"So it really exists?" I smiled and she looked at me with her eyes full of fun.

"Of course, it exists. It's out in the Atlantic off the

West of Ireland. It's not on any map you might see nowa-
days, but if you stand on the mountains of Connemara,
you can imagine that you see it sometimes, if the light is
just right."

She sighed.

"I think you can find it anywhere . . . perhaps in your
own heart . . . if you're lucky enough."

"There's a legend attached to it, isn't there?" I prompted
her. "A version of Rip Van Winkle."

"It's a wonderful story. It's about Oisin, the son of Finn.
The daughter of the King of Tir-nan-oge fell in love with
Oisin and she took him away to Tir-nan-oge on her white
steed. It was a lovely land with 'an abundance of gold and
silver and jewels, of honey and wine.' I had a book all
about it, when I was a child. The Princess gave Oisin a
hundred swords and a hundred keen-scented hounds, and
herds of cows without number and flocks of sheep with
fleeces of pure gold."

"You sound as if you believed it really happened." I
teased her and she looked at me for a moment.

"What's there to prove it didn't?" she asked me, and I
laughed at her.

"Well if it did, Oisin was a very lucky fellow," I
remarked. "I suppose that he lived happily ever after?"

She shook her head and pretended to be very sad.

"Indeed he did not. Like all men, he wasn't content
with what he found. He married the Princess, whose name,
by the way was 'Niam of the Golden Hair,' and he lived
with her in Tir-nan-oge for three hundred years. Of course,
it was only like three years to Oisin, because of the fairies'
magic. Then he wanted to see his father again and all his
old companions and poor Niam was very sad. She told

him that all his people were dead and gone, but he wouldn't believe her, and she saw that she must let him return to Erin and see for himself that what she said was true. She knew he loved her and that he'd come back to her and she gave him her white steed to carry him over the sea, but she warned him that he must on no account set foot on his native land, for if he did, he'd never be able to return to Tir-nan-oge any more."

"Oh, dear!" I said. "I can imagine what happened next. Poor Oisin saw an old woman picking sticks and got off his horse to help her. I seem to remember hearing a story like that once, but I didn't believe it, once I went to my Prep School."

"You gain nothing the day you learn there's no Father Christmas," she said. "But you lose a great deal."

"I believe it all implicitly," I told her. "I wasn't doubting its truth for one moment. Tell me the rest of it."

Her lashes fanned a dark shadow on her cheeks as she went on solemnly.

"She warned him three times that he must not get down from the white steed and he galloped straight down to the shore and away across the sea till he came to Erin, and there he found it all, just as she'd told him. The people there were not the ones he knew, and they told him of the great deeds of Finn, the mighty warrior and his son, Oisin, who had been dead, they said for three hundred years. So he turned the white steed to go back to Tir-nan-oge and as he came to the edge of the sea, he saw a great number of men trying to lift a big slab of stone. They had lifted it half up from the ground and they could get it no further and the men underneath were almost certain to be crushed to death, and Oisin was a powerful warrior. He leaned down from the saddle and lifted the stone and threw it seven perches from its place, but with the strain the girth of the saddle broke and he fell from the steed. The books say that it reared and was gone, 'like a cloud shadow on a March day.' "

She sighed again and looked at me and I shook my head sorrowfully.

"And Oisin felt his sight grow dim and his skin grow old and wrinkled and yellow as a duck's webbed foot and he fell to the ground an old man," she said.

"There's a tragedy for you," I agreed. "Think what a Musical you could make of it, but you'd have to have a happy ending, so you'd best tell me the rest of it. How did he find his way back to Tir-nan-oge?"

"He never found his way back," she said. "He lived out the dregs of his life, dreaming of Niam of the Golden Hair, knowing that the gates of Paradise were closed to him for ever . . . knowing that Niam was lonely for him in Tir-nan-oge and that her heart was broken too."

I looked at the red-gold of the setting sun.

"I think it might well have happened just like that," I told her. "I think it might happen like that today. A man might blunder into a place of enchantment and not have the wisdom to be content with it. He might go away and find out that he'd lost the way back for ever."

"And that's enough story-telling for one day," she said as severely as any school ma'am, as she picked up her book to ask me a speech I knew as well as I knew my own name.

I made a great show of finding it all very difficult . . . especially any passage with a hint of romance to it. I wonder that she did not notice how such parts had to be repeated and repeated again. I scowled, as I pretended I had forgotten a line. I took the book from her hand several times to see if I got the same electric shock, when I touched her and it never seemed to fail.

"It won't be easy on stage," she said in a serious way, that I found entrancing. "You'll be terrified of the audience and you won't remember a single line at first. We'll prompt you. Don't worry. I'll be there to help you and we'll leave the script lying about on-stage, where you can get a look at it from time to time. There are all kind of tricks of the theatre you'll have to learn."

I looked at her wise young face and knew well that one day, she would have to know who I was. I hoped that she would forgive my base deception, for I was well aware that I had found the thing, for which I had searched so long. I was in love with her inescapably and eternally and my only hope of happiness lay in making her love me too. She took my hand eventually and led me in to old Joshua and told him that I was very quick at learning the part. Then she sat herself down at my feet and listened, as I started my campaign, although she knew nothing about it.

"The television will never kill the living theatre," I began. "A picture in a box would never put any show off the road, if only that show was good enough."

We discussed this for a while and then I shot my second bolt.

"Do you ever have Mr. Barldrop dressed up in full Highland regalia to give the audience some of the old Scots tunes as an overture, instead of a record?" I asked. "He'd look pretty impressive, walking up and down the centre aisle of the theatre, and the Scottish folk are fond of the pipes."

They were all amazed that they had never thought of it before.

"They're an erudite people too," I went on, as if I had just thought of it. You could use Punch as a curtain raiser. Mr. Mardall could come out in front and give a short history of Punchinello . . . how he was introduced into England by a troupe of Italian players in 1660, and then the curtain could go up on Mr. Punch. Everybody loves a Punch and Judy Show."

They were very enthusiastic about it, and I had pushed myself forward enough for one day. I would have to hasten slowly . . . . I put my suggestions out one by one very patiently in the days, that followed.

"Why not get new costumes with the insurance money on the car wreck? I know a man in London, who has a place where you can get stuff for next to nothing. Some of the things are second hand, but you'd never know."

I took the few pounds that old Joshua gave me so trustingly and hoped that they would not notice that the costumes must have cost twenty times that amount.

"There's a chap called Bert Hollidge," I went on later. "He used to be a good stage manager, but he's got arthritis and he's down on his luck. He'd be very grateful, if you could find a place for him. He'd pull his weight too. I'd only have to phone him and he'd come like a shot. It's broken his heart to have to give up the stage . . . writes a bit too. He could write us some fresh material . . . Scottish stuff . . . extracts from the life of Robbie Burns . . . Robert, the Bruce, . . . Bonnie Prince Charlie. They'd love it and he'd only want his keep, unless we got going well. He could bring up the costumes too . . . save a lot of time if he travelled with them."

We moved on to Laragh at the end of the week and I managed not to kill myself and the entire company by running the bus over a precipice. Juliet sat at my side and coached me in my part, but for once, I was absent-minded. Miss Kiddle had burst a bomb under my feet before she drove away in her Austin Seven, with Dog Toby looking back from the window at me, wagging his tail. She had handed me a small key.

"Your more oppulent possessions are locked in the chest under the bed in the cottage," she said with a sly smile. "I don't know what part you're playing this season, Mr. Jonathan Harley, but you're a man of honour and I trust you. Your guilty secret is safe with me."

I had controlled my face as best I could.

"I don't know what you're talking about . . . . " I started, but she was not going to waste time like that.

"Oh, yes, you do. And don't worry. I won't tell on you."

"How did you find out?" I asked her stubbing my toe in the turf.

"You were rehearsing with Juliet outside the door last night and I couldn't see you. I heard your voice and it was as familiar as my own. I got it, when you told her you'd be happy if she was there to help you. What's he gone all husky about now? I thought. That's not an emotional line. Then I had it."

"Oh, dear!" I sighed.

"Don't break her heart," she said quietly. "She's young and defenceless."

"I won't break her heart," I said and met her eye squarely.

"And don't break her neck either," she fired off as a parting shot. "You're likely not used to driving buses."

We played the week out at Laragh and Jamie drove over in the Land Rover and watched Apryl act the part of Nerissa. I got a great amount of amusement out of my first appearance on any stage in Great Britain and they united in telling me that I showed great promise.

Sam Barldrop dressed up in a kilt and plaid and gave us pipe music each night as an overture, and we tried out the Punch and Judy Show as a curtain raiser and it was very popular. We moved on to the next small town and Bert Hollidge arrived, sworn to secrecy and threw himself into the campaign.

Of course, I could never have achieved all I did achieve, if it had not been for Miss Kiddle. She was my co-conspirator and my ally and my stout friend. There was Westlake in London too, at the end of the telephone to deal with that part of it.

After Bert Hollidge arrived, it was all very much simpler. If I happened to think of any bright ideas, it was Bert who introduced them. He was like a dog with two tails to be back in harness again. He even cast Apryl Barldrop in a ballet sequence, that was far in advance of anything the Players had ever attempted. It was very simple and delighted Apryl above everything and made her take the theatre seriously.

Meggie sat centre front and told my fortune. We used some of the net floats for decor and Meggie had one of them lighted up as a crystal ball. As she spoke the future came to life on the stage behind us in a ballet sequence. The dark lady . . . the Queen of Spades came on and danced a love sequence and what Miss Kiddle made as a costume for Apryl had to be seen to be believed. She had the black tights as foundation of course, but she had floating black chiffon and the playing card motif on her chest and back. Even I was astounded with Bert Hollidge that night.

Then he conceived the idea of having me read Robbie Burns from the right front, dressed in costume. On the stage behind me, poor Highland Mary was seen miming the wedding scene with her faithless lover, or in some similar scene . . . very simple to do but tremendously effective, and of course, the lovely poetry of Burns entranced the Highland audience. Somebody came out from one of the bigger towns and booked the show for a week and we inched our way upwards step by step.

It was Bert who told old Joshua about Ann Perry. Ann was in trouble, he said . . . one of the best actresses on the stage, forced to housekeep for a surly old man in Surbiton, because she would not put her little girl into a home. In two days, the cast was joined by Ann Perry and then we really got the thing moving and I had paid some of my debt to Hollidge and Miss Perry, for they were very happy.

Bert manhandled the three green juniors into shape . . . brutally and unmercifully. He took no notice of Apryl's flirtatious approach, nor Cedric's facetiousness, nor my lady's sulks. He rehearsed them all day and every day, and Miss Kiddle began to paste up her bills in bigger towns and there were advance bookings for bigger towns still, and we began to cast round in our minds, Bert and Ann and I, of what new blood to take into the Company.

I had wooed Juliet with tenderness, trying not to rush into a declaration of my love for her, and withstanding the temptation to tell her who I was and pick her up and carry her off to London with me. I thought that she loved me too. Often, I caught her looking at me with a soft expression in her eyes and we were always together. We walked for miles across the heather, hand in hand, making plans for the future, when I would be a great actor. I kissed her hand and her cheek and put an arm about her, and I was sad because I knew that time was running out. Westlake was badgering me to return to town at once, as the rehearsals for Bothwell had started and they wanted me. There was no delaying the opening night. "Surely that beard must be grown to perfection by now?" Westlake said on the phone.

I went into her dressing-room one night after the final curtain, having stationed Hermione Kiddle to guard the door like a watch dog. I knew that I must go up to town in a day or two and my heart was very heavy about having to leave Juliet.

I sat on the edge of the table and watched her cream her make-up off and I sighed as I borrowed the cream to take off my own.

"There's an end to the masquerade," I said.

She smiled up at me and told me that I was very serious all of a sudden.

"I want to have a talk with you," I said slowly. "A serious and very earnest talk."

She laughed at me and thought that I was joking.

"Was Bert not satisfied with me tonight? At least he can't say anything to you, your Majesty, for you were magnificent."

"You know that I'm not quite what I pretend to be," I said, "There's mystery about me and I've been hiding from something."

She laughed again.

"So at last I'm to hear the secret?"

I did not answer her for a long time and then my voice was troubled.

"First of all, I'm going to ask you to have faith in me."

"I have faith in you now. Absolute, complete and entire faith. You even prompted me once tonight, when I got stuck."

"Off stage," I said. "I've got to leave the Strolling Players."

The brightness was wiped from her eyes.

"For good?" she whispered and I nodded my head.

"I'm not necessary to the Show any longer. Bert Hollidge will look after you and you have Joshua and the others. We've planned to bring new blood into the cast in a few weeks and there's no possibility of failure at this stage. You can get along without me."

"I can't get along without you," she said, before she could stop herself and I was filled with great joy.

I took her hand in mine and bent my head to kiss it and hold it against my cheek.

"I love you very much."

"Do you?" she murmured. "Do you?"

"I shall go on loving you for ever," I went on. "I would be very honoured indeed if you would become my wife."

She raised her brows at me.

"Your wife, your Majesty?"

I went away across the room from her and stood and studied a poster on the wall, as if it were a thing of vital importance.

"I'm a man without a name. I'll tell you in a month or two all about myself and how I landed up in Tir-nan-oge, but I'd like you to promise me you'll marry me, before

I tell you about it."

"So I'm to buy a pig in a poke?"

"If you wish to put it like that."

"So you're a man of great wealth and power?" she laughed. "You want me to love you for yourself alone, as they say in the story books, and not because you're the most famous actor in the British Isles, especially when you play Romeo? Did you think I didn't know?"

I spun round and looked at her in amazement, and then I saw that she had only said it in fun.

"You know Meggie told us that you were a man of great talent, who would go to the top of his profession," she reminded me with a smile. "You're acting was so good tonight, that I really think we'll make something of you. Perhaps you'll be a great actor one day."

"A pig in a poke," I reminded her.

"But a very nice and royal pig, your Majesty, whom I love very much indeed and shall continue to do so, 'Till a' the seas gang dry.' "

I went on my knees at her feet and put my arms about her full skirts and buried my face against her and could not speak, if I had been killed for my silence. She stroked my hair gently and ran her fingers along my bearded jaw.

"Is the beard to come off then?"

I shook my head.

"I'm glad," she sighed. "I like it. It makes you look like Robin Devereaux, Earl of Essex."

I stood up and took her into my arms.

"And who is Robin Devereaux, Earl of Essex?" I demanded.

Her eyes sparkled with fun, full of the little silver fish of mischief and her white teeth were as evenly matched as a string of pearls.

"I played him at school once. I put on the beard with spirit gum. It was awfully hard to get it off again."

I kissed her cheek gently.

"I'm glad you managed it," I whispered in her ear. "It was an impertinence to put it on such a chin in the first place."

"Was it?" she teased me. "They said it became me very well."

I kissed her warm soft lips and knew what it was to walk on the golden plains of Tir-nan-oge, the land of eternal happiness.

We stayed in the dressing-room for so long that we got into trouble with Meggie, but we told them the news and that I must go away very soon, but that I would return within two months, when we planned to get married.

"I hope you know what you're doing," Miss Kiddle said, as they saw me off on the train two days later. "You're going about things in a mighty peculiar manner. If I'd been you, I'd have told her all about it, straight out."

I picked her up in my arms and kissed her, before I put her down again. I told her that she was a deceitful old rogue and not to be trusted for one moment, and then I kissed my lovely Juliet goodbye and turned my face towards the south.

I travelled down to Euston from Edinburgh in my old corduroy jacket and a pair of very disreputable slacks with all my luggage in a knapsack. My more opulent possessions were still reposing in the locked case under the bed in the cottage. My compartment had been reserved for a Mr. John and the attendant had no idea that he was entertaining Jonathan Harley, now on his way to London to appear as James Hepburn, Lord Bothwell in a show, that was already booked out for the first four weeks.

Westlake met me with the car and I was very gratified, when he passed my by on the platform without a second glance and went walking along the train with his eyes still searching for me.

I went out and sat in the car and waited for him, with a grin like a Cheshire cat's on my face. It was parked in its usual place and after a while he came back looking rather dejected, with a faintly worried expression. He saw me as he opened the door.

"Weel met, Mr. Westlake!" I cried. "Dinna ye recognize an auld friend aifter a' these lang weeks?"

"My God! I passed you by on the platform," he ejaculated. "I thought you were a down-and-out painter from Chelsea and I wondered what on earth you were doing getting out of a first class sleeper. I hoped that you hadn't stolen anything."

"Thank you very much," I said drily. "That augers well for the Earl of Bothwell."

He got in behind the wheel, turning to study me.

"The face is fine. It's those scarecrow clothes of yours. You'll have to part with that jacket now, at any rate. Have you been sleeping rough in the ditches? Your costume is eminently suited for the dustbin, but that beard's damned good."

"I'm relieved that you approve of that at least," I

laughed as he edged the car out into the traffic.

He glanced at me for a moment.

"I approve of a lot more than the beard. You've done a good job, J.H. . . . a damned good job. I don't know that you've had much of a holiday, but you've given a creditable performance one way and another. You've put quite a few people back into the sun again, without costing the discomfort and sacrifice you made yourself."

I watched the crowded pavements flash past the car window.

"I got a very clear picture of Jonathan Harley," I said slowly. "I had what I suppose you might call a revelation. It happened on a rocky sea shore near Tir-nan-oge, after a spotty youth, who fancied himself as a comic, had saved my life. I saw myself clearly for the first time and I didn't think much of what I saw. I hope I'm a reformed character, but I'm not sure."

"And did you apologize to the Queen of Scotland?" he asked me. "You know that you lost that bet. You only stayed two weeks in the cottage."

"Do you know that it quite slipped my mind," I told him. "I'll get round to it one of these days, but I couldn't seem to find the right moment."

"But you told her who you were, before you came away? Surely you could have done it then?"

"I didn't tell her. I couldn't find the moment for that either. I'll send them some tickets for the first night of the show and let them find it out for themselves, when the tabs go up."

He pulled the car to a halt outside the flat.

"That's a dramatic way of doing it," he laughed. "But I don't know what her Majesty will say. She can't hold much brief for Harley, you know."

"Can't she though?" I told him. "She's going to marry him, as soon as the show goes on. He's head over heels in love with her and she says she loves him too. What's in a name? She loves me. Ergo, she loves Harley."

"She loves you?" he cried. "Good God! You're not going to break the news to her like that? With all the others . . . in a crowded theatre. Oh, no, J.H. That wouldn't be wise at all."

We went up to the flat and I marvelled at the elegance of my possessions. I put on a dark town suit and a cream silk shirt and I looked at myself in the glass, as I brushed my hair, but I hardly recognized myself.

"After all," I said suddenly to Westlake, who was sitting on the edge of the bed with a notebook on his knee, giving me the latest news of the production. "After all, I have so much more to offer her as Jonathan Harley. If she loved me, when I had nothing, she must love me far more, as I really am."

I was trying to convince myself, not him and he was not convinced. He looked at me gloomily.

"It depends on her sense of values. 'Pity is sworn servant unto love.' Nobody could pity Harley."

I threw the brushes out of my hands with a clatter and turned to him in exasperation.

"And what would you do in my place?"

I should go up to Scotland and tell her the whole story and throw myself on her mercy. You'll likely have made a fool of her one way and another, if I know you. For one thing, I imagine you let her believe that you'd never been on a stage before and presumably, she thought she helped you quite a bit.

I laughed and came over to look down at him.

"If you knew the fun I had. She used to teach me all my parts . . . took me under her wing. She was my greatest champion. The others thought I was pretty bad, but she said that I'd make a good actor one day."

"That's precisely what I mean," he said. "She's a sensitive girl and very easily hurt. You've offended her once and she'll likely think that you thought the whole thing a great joke."

I argued with him and told him that of course, she would understand. She would be just as amused at it in retrospect as I was. She had a terrific sense of humour. She would laugh her head off about it.

"I hope so," he said and went off out of the room, but he was disaproving of me again.

I could tell it by the way he held his shoulders.

I met my new leading lady that night. She came to the flat with Salvage, the play-wright, and Sally Druce came along too, to make up the party. Salvage had a new play running in the West End with Sally in the female lead and Westlake hinted to me that there was a romantic attachment between them. Sally and Salvage arrived together straight from the theatre and Sally took one look at me, where I stood with my back to the fire, talking to my leading lady and held out both hands to me.

"Darling Johnnie!" she cried, and ran across the room into my arms. "You're three times as attractive as you were before. You handsome, wonderful man!"

She flung her arms about my neck and I smelt the familiar pared-pencil sophistication of her scent. She kissed me and I saw that Salvage was not very happy about it, so I got away from her as soon as I could and went over to sit beside the dark girl, whom we had brought over from the Gate Theatre Company in Dublin to play Mary, Queen of Scots. She was an oval-faced, pale-skinned beauty with all the softness and gentleness of the Irish skies in her voice. She had an unpronounceable Gaelic name, that none of our tongues could manage with any degree of accuracy, so we called her Susan.

I had met her that night for the first time and I thought she would do well for the part. She was the opposite in everything to my late Ophelia . . . shy, reticent and rather over-awed by the thought of her first appearance on the London stage. She had been over for two weeks for the preliminary rehearsals, so she knew Salvage and Sally.

"You're from Ireland," I smiled at her. "You'll know all about Tir-nan-oge. It's the name of Sally's cottage in Scotland, where I've been hiding to grow this beard."

For some reason, I pretended to know nothing of the legend and asked her to tell it to us and I got a melancholy satisfaction in hearing the story all over again. When she had finished, I told her that of course, I believed it all implicitly and she looked at me with laughter in the back of her grey eyes.

"They told me you were a dreamer," she smiled. "I hope that we'll get on well together."

"Of course we shall," I promised her. "We'll bring the Royal Court of Scotland to life again. We'll let them live a little and love a little and then we'll put them back between the pages of the history books, knowing that they're not forgotten."

Salvage was very taken with the legend of Tir-nan-oge and Sally was trying to persuade him to write a play for her.

"I could play 'What's-it of the Golden Hair.' " she pouted at him. "At least you'd approve of a blond for that and we could see if they'd believe in fairies in Piccadilly."

I plunged into rehearsals the next day and into all the staging of a West End production, but no matter how my time was occupied, Juliet haunted all my days . . . and all my nights too.

Salvage might start to argue about some question of the dialogue and there I would be, back in Scotland again with the Strolling Players and old Joshua, snuff-box in hand, would be pontificating to Juliet and myself on some point of theatre.

Susan reminded me of her continually, I would catch a glimpse of her dark head or a gesture of a hand and for a second, she would be Juliet, before I realized, with a strange desolation, that I had wandered far from Tir-nan-oge. Sometimes, when I went back to the flat in the evening, I fancied that she had been there and had just left. It was as if I heard her light sigh, felt her breath on my cheek, smelt the fragrance of her hair. At night, I had dreams, where she appeared beside me, always on the stage on some night-mare of a play, where nothing went right. She would vanish and always I followed her and searched for her and never found her and only woke up at last in an emptiness of spirit and an aching desolation, as I knew she was lost to me forever.

I had been to work behind the scenes of the theatre-world on behalf of the Strolling Players the day after my return to town. It was easy enough to do and I did not get them any position, that they were not eminently capable of filling.

I had heard that the Arts Council wanted to finance a tour of plays for the Scottish Islands during the next summer and the Players were tailor-made for the task. All I had to arrange was that they would get an audition in London during the week we opened with JAMES HEPWORTH, EARL OF BOSWELL, and they would be there with the full cast. It should have been a simple thing to write a letter to Miss Hemingway, enclosing complimentary tickets for our first night, but I tore up twenty drafts of that letter, before I got one that I thought was adequate . . . and all the time, the certainty was growing in my mind that Westlake had been right. I was making a fool of myself and my whole stratagem must end in failure.

The weeks of rehearsal dragged on for what seemed a million years and ten days before the opening, I sent the letter off.

"Dear Miss Hemingway, you were kind enough to call at my flat some months ago and ask me to appear with your company, but unfortunately I was prevented from doing this, by circumstances beyond my control. I have never apologized that I did not see you personally that day, though I will make it my business to see you in the near future and do so.

As some kind of redress for my boorish behaviour, I am sending you seats for our new show and I would be honoured if you would accept them. Also, I'd be flattered if you could come backstage afterwards, so that I can congratulate you personally on the good entertainment you are providing for the Scots theatre . . . and of course, to make that belated apology and cast myself upon your mercy . . . . "

If I possessed any sense in my head, I should have written a vastly different letter . . . one that explained who I was and how it had come about that I found myself a member of the Strolling Players . . . one that told her I loved her and would love her till the day I died. However, I adhered to my romantic notion of appearing before her as Jonathan Harley in the newest and most publicised play in London, though all my self-confidence was running away like water through a sieve.

In four days, I got her reply.

"Dear Mr. Harley, I was surprised to get your letter and to know that you had not forgotten all about my visit. You must have many calls upon your valuable time. It is indeed a generous reparation on your part to send us seats for the opening night and we are all very excited at the thought of seeing your show and wish you every success with it. Sincerely yours, Juliet Hemingway . . . . "

I read it a hundred times and was illogically disappointed every time that she had not sent her love to me and that shows the state of my mind. This was the only communication we made with each other, for she had decreed quite firmly that it would be best if we did not write to each other. It was not, she explained, that she would ever change her mind about loving me, but she wanted time for me to reflect, uninfluenced by letters passing between us, so that I could be really sure that I wanted her for my bride . . . and now, I sat at my desk with this letter in my hand and was sad because she did not send her love to Jonathan Harley, whom she did not know from Adam . . . .

I do not know what my leading lady made of me during the last week before the dress rehearsal, for I hardly opened my mouth to her except when I spoke my lines. Presumably she concluded that I was working up to first night nerves. She could have no idea that every hour of my day was filled with my conviction that Juliet would consider Jonathan Harley a different being from Mr. John . . . that she would come and see me and go away again.

On the day of the dress rehearsal, I was sitting out front, in the full regalia of my costume in my own private slough of depression, when Susan came to sit beside me.

"They tell me you're always on edge about first nights, but you mustn't worry about tomorrow."

I turned my head to look at the pale oval of her face and wondered what she would say if I told her what was really worrying me.

"It can't go wrong, Jonathan . . . not with Salvage's play . . . not with you as Bothwell. You're an inspiration to the rest of us, you know. You carry us all along with you to greatness on your own broad shoulders."

"And now you're talking kind nonsense," I said moodily, but she would not have it, and I argued with her.

"I'd be pretty helpless without you and the others . . . a mere Punchinello, full of sawdust. One person doesn't count much one way or the other and I'm not particularly proud of myself."

She took my hand in hers and looked down at the great

ring on my finger.

"You've every right to be proud of yourself, my lord Bothwell. Don't ever think otherwise. It's all words . . . dead words written on paper and then you come on. Don't you know that with your entry, time moves back four hundred years . . . and we live it all again? It really happens. You must be aware of it. I've never worked with anybody remotely like you. I knew about you of course. Everybody knows the reputation you've won . . . and rightly won."

I looked up at the brightly-lit stage at the boudoir set and saw the Queen's tiring women and the ladies in waiting, like a cluster of rich jewels and the little jingle ran through my head.

> "Yestreen the Queen had four Maries
> The night, she'll hae but three . . . .
> There was Marie Seaton and Marie Beaton
> And Marie Carmichael and me . . . . "

"You'd better go," I warned her. "You're on in three minutes."

She bent towards me, her voice soft and earnest.

"I've never known anybody like you. Thank you for what you've done for me. It's been a great honour to play opposite you and I'll never forget the way you've helped me . . . not to my dying day."

She lifted my hand to her face and held it for a moment against her soft cheek, in just the manner that Juliet used to do it.

"Don't be unhappy about the opening tomorrow. You won't fail . . . never . . . never . . . never. You're patterned to success, my lord."

It was too late to change my mind now. There was no time to travel to Scotland and throw myself on Juliet's mercy. The Strolling Players would already be on their way south, for they were due to arrive just before the show opened and I knew the hotel where they planned to stay. There was no escape now from my dramatic revelation of my identity. I was condemned to go through with it and I knew in my heart that it had been a foolish notion. I cursed myself at this late stage, that I had not listened to Westlake's wisdom . . . and the dress rehearsal ran away far too smoothly. I got back to the flat late at night and tumbled into bed and then sleep eluded me, so that I lay and stared at the dancing lights on the ceiling and wondered where Juliet was and if she lay awake and thought of me too. Then suddenly I was in a deep and dreamless sleep and when I awoke, there was Westlake standing beside the bed with a glass of orange juice in his hand and my dressing gown over his arm.

"The great day is here, J.H. and there are a hundred and one details awaiting your attention."

I swung my legs out of bed and sat with my head in my hands, till Westlake reminded me there was no time for such luxuries. Then I sat up and took the glass out of his hand and soon I had had a shower and was dressed and the time was running through my hands like quicksilver. It was lunch time . . . tea-time . . . the hours were all gone and the darkness had come down again.

"It's time we were leaving for the theatre, J.H. Courage, mon brave!"

I arrived in my dressing room an hour and a half before the tabs were due to go up, thinking that before the night was over, I would see Juliet again and talk to her. I would tell her how it had come about that I had met her in Lismore, tell her that I was the same foolish fellow as Mr. John . . . tell her that I loved her very dearly, and then await her decision.

Bill gave me a sheaf of telegrams of goodwill and I flung them down on the table and then got superstitious and went through them all, for who was I, that I did not need good luck tonight?

Bill helped me to get dressed and I stood and looked at my reflection in the glass and saw the rich brocade cloth of the doublet and slashed hose . . . the high black collar, with the lace ruff dramatically white at its edge, the heavy gold chain about my neck and dangling in a double coil to my waist.

My heart was beating fast as I sat down before my bench and prepared to put on my make up. Outside the theatre the audience would be gathering in and gathering in from all the corners of the city. There was no unbooked seat in the auditorium and now they would be coming, by bus, by train, by car, on foot. It was a thought, that never failed to terrify me. I wondered where Juliet was and Joshua Mardall, Sam and Maggie, Cedric and Apryl, Bert Hollidge, Ann Perry. They were unreal to me. I could not see them in this setting. It was as if they had never been . . . as if they were creatures of my imagination. I thought that perhaps I had dreamt it all and that I could never recapture the dream, if I searched all my life. Tonight, perhaps I should face Juliet here in this room and hear her verdict on Jonathan Harley . . . that is, if she ever existed at all.

I sent Westlake out front tot he foyer to watch for them and make them welcome. He knew the fears that possessed me and put a hand on my shoulder before he left.

"Don't worry about it. You have enough on your mind with the show. It'll come out happily for you, and good luck, J.H. with both ventures!"

I put on my own make-up, as I always preferred to do and afterwards the make up man came round and discussed it with me and pretended that he did not notice how my hands were shaking.

"Ten minutes, Mr. Harley," said the call boy.

I sent Bill out once again to see if the seats were taken, and when he came back and told me that they were still vacant, I felt real panic grip me in the stomach. Three minutes later, I sent him out again and he came back and shook his head and bent down to put a polish on my long thigh boots, that were already polished to perfection.

"Two minutes, Mr. Harley."

The producer would have gone out front by now, having examined the stage and passed it as correct.

I got up and felt that my legs were two bolsters of feathers and I tried to pull myself together. I tried to remember my opening lines and it was all confusion. I could only see Juliet standing in my dressing room, telling me it was all over.

"Stand by for tabs."

Bill opened the door and came along to open the pass door to the stage. I read the familiar notice, as if I had never seen it before.

STAGE. CAST AND STAFF ONLY. NO SMOKING ALLOWED. SILENCE.

As always, I wanted to turn and run away down the stairs . . . to hail a taxi and go back home . . . to lock myself in my room and put my head in my hands and hole out from the world, who were waiting out front to tear me to pieces.

I stood in the wings and felt the electricity, that pervaded the whole theatre.

"House lights out."

"They're still not taken, sir," said Bill at my side. "Those seats I was watching."

I looked at the Court of Scotland arrayed on-stage . . . Mary on her golden throne of state with Darnley standing ready to flirt with one of the ladies in waiting, as soon as the tabs went up . . . .

The words of the old ballad went round and round in my head again.

> "Yestreen the Queen had four Maries
> The night she'll hae but three,
> There was Marie Seaton and Marie Beaton
> And Marie Carmichael and me . . . . "

I looked at the two huge guards in armour that stood by the door and then the curtain was sliding up and the applause came over the floats as the audience took in the magnificence of the set.

The first lines of the play were being spoken and I had forgotten everything except that Juliet had not come. I knew I could never play my part with that thought in my head. It went over and over all mixed up in a crazy way with the ballad and I could feel the palms of my hands wet with sweat.

Craig, the stage-manager was at my side, grinning as usual.

"This is the worst moment, my lord. It'll be soon over."

I turned to tell him to get my understudy on and then I clenched my fists and heard Salvage's dialogue going on and on for ever. My cue was coming. I should be round by the door at the rear of the stage, but I did not move.

Susan's clear laughter came rippling across to the wings. Then one of the ladies-in-waiting spoke.

"James Hepburn, the Earl of Bothwell is in the antechamber and craves an audience, your majesty."

Susan laughed again and her voice was as musical and as clear as a bell.

"Then let him cool his heels for half an hour. Perhaps they've taught him patience in the Tower, though we doubt it. My lord, Bothwell was never a patient man and he's too proud and arrogant by half. What say you, Henry? Shall we let him await our pleasure and bring his pride low?"

Her husband, Darnley moved over from Marie Hamilton to stand behind her chair of state and his hand came down to her smooth cheek. I moved round to the entrance, listening to Darnley's voice.

"Are you not afraid that he'll murder your guards and kick the doors down, my darling? You know he got free when they clapped him in the dungeons here in Edinburgh and now it seems that not even Bess's great prison can hold him. Besides, you've recalled him to your side. It's small wonder he's impatient. What man would not haste to be with you?"

"Indeed my lord, you speak with a soft tongue. Let him come in then, for we are melancholy today and our heart is heavy with foreboding. Perhaps he'll bring a smile to our lips from the Tower, though 'tis no merry place."

I thought suddenly of Apryl Barldrop and the opening line of the Spanish Lady.

"I don't know why I'm so sad today."

I smiled as I remembered Cedric at rehearsals doing his little tap dance on the creaking boards of the stage and saying, "Thou hast butterflies in thy stomach, O sister mine," and what Bert Hollidge said to them and then I got my cue and was on.

"There was surprise, that went up all over the theatre like a sigh for two seconds, as they saw the beard. They must have seen the pictures outside the foyer, but still there was a pause, before the great wave of applause. I bowed deeply to her Majesty and then to Darnley and went over to kneel at the Queen's feet and kiss her hand. The rings glinted on her fingers, as she put a cool hand against my cheek and smiled at me.

"Why, Jamie. You've grown thin and pale since we last saw you. Did the sun not filter through to that prison-house of yours?"

I smiled up at her and heard my own voice.

"There is no sun away from your Majesty's presence. Life is grey when I go from you and when I return, the sun is shining and the sky is blue. I promise you that my face will not be so white after a day or two at your side."

She was laughing again.

"You speak with a soft tongue too. All our fine gentle-men speak with soft tongues and yet there is a shadow on our heart today. Can it be that you are a bird of ill omen, Jamie, come to carry disaster upon the Royal House of Scotland?"

I was standing by now and had glanced at the row of empty seats in the stalls. Perhaps Westlake would have some message from them. I would see him, when I went back to the dressing-room. The act was running very smoothly, but I was not James Hepburn, Earl of Bothwell. For the first time in my life, I was Jonathan Harley on stage and I was worried out of my wits, because my lady had not come. I had a conviction that, like Oisin, I was locked out of Tir-

nan-oge for all time, with no hope of finding the white
steed to carry me back to happiness.

Westlake was sitting in the wings as the tabs came down
on the first act. He came along to my dressing room and
sent Bill off on some pretext or another.

"They came," he told me as soon as we were alone.
"They came, but they went away again."

"They went away again?" I echoed foolishly.

"It was a most peculiar thing," he went on. "I didn't see
them personally. I hung about in the foyer for three quart-
ers of an hour and I couldn't have missed them with your
description. Besides, I'd have recognized that girl anywhere.
Then I remembered that picture of yours out front. I sent
for the door-man and he'd seen them. They arrived about a
quarter to. He said it was an odd thing. He didn't see them
coming. They appeared from nowhere. He turned round
and there they were.

I sat down and put my head in my hands.

"I suppose he wasn't mistaken?" I muttered, but I knew
only too well that there had been no mistake.

"I asked him to describe them to me and he said there
was this dwarf lady, but he had the others too and he
knew Bert Hollidge and Miss Perry. They had a word with
him and told him that they were in a new show some place
up north. He was surprised to see Bert Hollidge. He
thought he was dead."

I pulled myself together and sat up to watch Westlake's
reflection in the mirror.

"They all clustered round the photographs outside the
door, the doorman told me. Bert and Miss Perry went over
to talk with him and then they went back to the pictures.
There was some sort of argument going on between them,

but it was all a bit of a mix up, because people were pushing and shoving all around the entrance."

"So she didn't want to have anything to do with Jonathan Harley?" I said in a flat voice. "She went away."

He looked down at the top of my head.

"I think it may be something quite different, J.H. Apparently, there was pretty free discussion going on in the crowd and one woman called out, "We're to see his new leading lady tonight. He picked a beauty .this time and they say he's going to get married at last. Ain't she the lucky lassie to marry the great Jonathan Harley?"

I looked at him incredulously.

"Juliet heard somebody say that I was going to marry Susan? Oh, no! That can't be true!"

"The door-man told me that when the woman said that, one of the girls . . . and it must have been Juliet . . . ran across the pavement and jumped into a cab, that had just unloaded a fare. She went off by herself without a word."

"She couldn't have believed that."

Westlake shook his head.

"Indeed she believed it. Why else did she run away like that?"

"So she's gone?" I said miserably.

"They're all gone," he told me. "The door-man said that he stood looking after her for a while and then another taxi came in and when he turned back to the place they'd been standing, they'd all vanished."

I met his eyes sadly in the glass as I started to touch up my make-up.

"You were right then. It wasn't a wise thing to do after all."

Bill knocked at the door and came in.

"For God's sake, Mr. Harley, let me get your change done. You'll be on again in a quarter of an hour. There isn't much time."

"It doesn't matter much, does it?" I asked him wearily.

"You'll have to hurry, sir."

"Come in then. Let's get it over. The show must go on, even though Punchinello is . . . . "

I gripped the edge of the bench with my fingers till my knuckles shone white.

"Can a puppet possess a heart, do you think, Westlake? Perhaps it's impossible. Perhaps it's all been a trick of the long Scottish evenings . . . a play of shadows on a screen with no reality to it. Good God! I don't even know if it ever happened or not."

Bill came across and began to help me out of the rich brocade doublet.

"I don't know what's got into you tonight, sir. Really I don't. One of the lads was out front just now and they're raving about the show . . . about your performance too. The ladies approve of the beard, if I may say so. They won't have you shave it off again at any price."

"Blast the ladies!" I said shortly. "Blast the show and blast my beard!"

Westlake was standing with his hands clasped together in front of him like a curate.

"Was it all a dream?" I demanded.

"You forget that I met the lady," he reminded me. "She was flesh and blood. There's no possible doubt of that. It seems that you've got another journey of reparation to make, J.H. I really think there's no reason to be so put out about it. You went about this in the wrong way, but you've done that with this particular lady before and come out of it with honour. It can be done again."

"But can it?" I demanded. "Can it? You said yourself that pity was sworn servant unto love. Nobody could pity Jonathan Harley, not as he is tonight in his latest blasted stage triumph with the whole blasted world at his feet, all except the one, who matters more than all the others."

He laughed as he went off towards the door.

"You're wrong there, you know. I think that the great Harley is greatly to be pitied. He's gained the whole world except the one treasure he prized above everything . . . the one thing he has waited for . . . hoped for . . . thought he possessed at last. That's the worst bitterness of all, but it will come out happily in the end . . . not like the legend of Tir-nan-oge. There's nothing the great man can't do, if only he goes about it the right way.

I went through the last two acts like a mechanical man. Nobody seemed to notice that I was not the Earl of Bothwell, who had won the love of his Queen and then lost it for ever. I suppose that Jonathan Harley had done just that and was a tolerable substitute for the part.

At last I was on stage, toeing the chalked line with the full company and then Susan and I were alone, and the tabs rose and fell, and rose and fell, running up and down so smoothly, that I thought of the curtains in the Parish Hall at Lismore and felt the miserable old feeling in the pit of my stomach. Then I was alone and the applause came flooding across the floats in a vast tide to overwhelm me. I stepped forward and made the speech, just as I had done it at rehearsals and then I was back in my dressing room, with Tim, the stage door-man, bringing yet another great artificial arrangement of stiff mixed flowers.

"I'll see no-one," I told him. "I'm not very well."

He looked at me with concern, as he handed me a note.

"This came for you, sir. It was left by a lovely little dwarf lady . . . no higher than my waist, but the nicest person you could wish to meet. She said I was to tell you to be sure not to worry . . . that worry killed the cat!"

I tore open the letter addressed to me in Miss Kiddle's precise hand.

"My dear Mr. John,
You played the act tonight under your own direction and it hasn't worked out. Juliet heard an aside not intended for her ears and thought you loved somebody else. Apart from that, it might have run well. Will you take a little direction now from a person, who never appears on any stage by the grace of God, and play it my way?

Don't waste your time trying to find your lady tonight, for she has gone into hiding and even I do not know where to find her, but I do know where she will be tomorrow . . . and tomorrow I'll come looking for you. Be ready to come with me. I'll take you to her and the best of luck will go with you.
Your sincere friend and admirer.
Hermione Kiddle."

There was a post-script and I could imagine the quirk of her mouth as she mocked herself.

"P.S. Even in real life, I don't appear on stage. It gives me a better view of the action of the greatest play of all."

I sent Bill off to find Westlake and I handed him the letter and he sat down on the bench before the make-up mirror and read it, while I told Bill to go out and pacify my visitors outside.

"That's it then," declared Westlake, when he had gone. "You'll just have to wait till tomorrow."

"Of course I won't wait till tomorrow. I'll find her to-night if it's the last thing I do. I'll go to this hotel, where they're staying and ask to see her."

He looked at me gloomily.

"They're not there any longer. I rang just now. They checked out their luggage and went off. The people at reception thought they had gone back to Scotland . . . . "

"Very well. I'll go to the station. I may be in time to catch them before there's a train."

"And what if you don't?"

"I'll go up to Scotland after them. I'll find her."

Westlake looked at me laconically now.

"There's another show tomorrow night . . . and the next night . . . and the night after that."

"What do I care?" I demanded and he smiled at me.

"You'd be letting down a great number of people. It would be far better to trust the little lady. They can't have gone out of town. Otherwise, she could not promise to bring you to Miss Hemingway tomorrow."

His hand came down on my shoulder.

"Better get that make-up off for a start," he suggested and I sat down and stared at my reflection in the mirror.

"Suppose I do find her and she won't see me? Suppose

she slams the door of Tir-nan-oge in my face and puts a Cherubim on guard outside it, with a flaming sword that turns every way to keep me out? What then?"

He laughed suddenly and clapped me on the back.

"Then you emulate Lord Bothwell. You stab the Cherubim and you kick the door down. Then you go and kneel before the Queen of Scotland."

"It's not as easy as that," I grumbled as I started to remove my make-up. "Remember Oisin, son of Finn. You don't get back to the enchanted land, if you've been fool enough to leave . . . and I was fool enough to leave."

He passed a fresh towel across to me and then sat himself down astride a chair and he was smiling still.

"You're not like Oisin. You'll find your way to enchantment again. There'll be no Cherubim with flaming sword or anything else . . . only your lady with her arms stretched out to you."

I unwound the heavy gold chain from about my neck and flung it down on the table.

"I'll go to the station now all the same and to their hotel. If they're still in town, I'll find them."

I unbuttoned my doublet and Westlake pulled off my thigh boots and then Bill's anxious face was peering round the door.

"There's a lot of your friends and well-wishers outside, sir. They won't be put off seeing you. Miss Druce and Mr. Salvage have planned a celebration that'll go on the whole night, and they're waiting for you."

"There's nothing to celebrate," I said shortly. "If they mean to celebrate, they'll do it without me."

Westlake had gone back to sit astride the chair with his chin down on his folded arms.

"Let's hope it'll be a different story tomorrow night," he sighed. "I have that license in my pocket book."

I was dressed at last and I told them that I would go out the front way. I slipped through the darkened theatre like a shadow. It was sordid with the litter of chocolate boxes and programmes and the air felt as if it had been breathed by a thousand throats. The doorman was surprised to see me, but he let me out and hailed a taxi for me and I was away before anybody had time to notice me. Then I followed my own inclinations and ignored Westlake's advice and Miss Kiddle's letter. I searched the station, going from one departure platform to the next and finding no sign of them in the teeming crowd of strangers. I looked in the waiting rooms and the refreshment places and questioned a few porters, but got no help from them. Then I took a taxi to the hotel and the girl at the reception desk looked at me suspiciously, before she recognized me and then she gushed and fawned and flattered, but could help me in no way about the Strolling Players, who had checked out and gone away hours before. She was a kind girl all the same and she telephoned a score of other hotels for me and drew a blank at each one and then I thanked her and went out and wandered about the streets, as I had done in my dreams, searching for her but never finding her. I was totally exhausted by the time I fell into bed, but the excitement of the night had keyed my nerves to screaming point and my brain became a screen for one picture after another. I turned on my face and buried my head in my pillow and still the pictures of unhappiness flapped over and flapped over like a mental magic lantern, till I wondered if I was going out of my mind. It was almost morning, when at last I went asleep and I did not wake till noon, when I found Westlake in the room, with a sheaf of papers under his arm.

"You've got wonderful notices, J.H. You've done it again. Salvage has been on the phone and Sally Druce and two dozen others. You've got a stack of letters too, delivered by hand . . . all congratulations . . . all acclaiming the great Jonathan Harley."

I sat up and grabbed the letters from the table by my head to scrabble through them feverishly.

"There isn't one from Miss Hemingway," Westlake told me mildly. "But I shouldn't worry about it. Pin your faith in Hermione Kiddle. She won't let you down."

He held my dressing gown out for me and I shrugged my shoulders into it and then he fished round in his waistcoat pocket and peered at me over his horn-rimmed spectacles.

"Incidentally . . . . "

He passed a ticket to me.

" . . . . This might be of interest to you. You left it in your desk that morning and it's been there ever since."

I looked down at the bad print on the cheap cardboard and was back in the Parish Hall at Lismore in a moment.

JOSHUA MARDALL'S COMPANY OF STROLLING PLAYERS INVITES YOU TO ATTEND ANY ONE OF THEIR PERFORMANCES IN ANY THEATRE, WHERE THEY MAY BE PLAYING. THIS TICKET WILL ADMIT ONE PERSON, WHO WILL BE CORDIALLY WELCOME.

I read her now-familiar hand across the face of it.

"I see, sir, you are generous in offers,
You taught me how to beg and now methinks
You teach me how a beggar should be answered . . . . "

I stood there and looked down at it for a long time and then I glanced over to Westlake.

"I had my horoscope done in a restaurant one evening I was out with Ophelia. There was a gypsy girl there and she told me I'd get a letter or a card . . . a piece of writing at any rate, that would seem of no importance at the time. She said that my happiness would depend upon it. I thought it was the usual sort of poppycock, but now I wonder. I got this the next day. Do you think . . . ?"

"I think it's a good luck piece of great value. Perhaps it's a ticket back into the land of enchantment, you seem so struck on finding . . . and now it's high time you had your breakfast for it's well past twelve and there's been a dress rehearsal called for two thirty. It seems there's some difficulty with the dresses and the action wasn't as smooth as it might have been. They want the full company in costume . . . . "

He grinned at my rueful face.

"Miss Kiddle can find you in the theatre. If she comes here, they'll direct her on, and by the way, J.H. in the excitement of your entry into paradise, don't forget you're on again tonight . . . and for God's sake, stop looking so unhappy. It will all work out in the finish. It was just your dramatic way of doing things that I questioned originally, but you always get away with that sort of thing. You'll win your fair lady. There's no possible doubt of that, but just for the moment, come and have your breakfast and read the press notices, there's a good chap."

By two o'clock, I was in the dressing room again, starting to put on the rich brocade costume. It took me a long time to get the high ruffle adjusted to my satisfaction, for my hands had started to shake again. I had had to send Bill across to Romanoff's to get the fastening adjusted on one of my doublets, so I was without his expert help and I cursed myself for my nervousness as I pulled on my boots and hung the double chain of gold about my neck. Last of all I slid the great ring on my finger and it caught the light in its single eye and winked at the brilliance of my sword hilt. Then Craig was at my side, meeting my eyes in the mirror and telling me that I would not be required for very long.

"The women's full skirts played the devil with us last night. They'll have to settle down and get used to handling them, but we'll only want you while we run through the first act."

By three thirty, I was through and striding off-stage and back to the sanctuary of my dressing room again. I flung the door open and looked down on the square pleasant face of Hermione Kiddle. She was sitting on the seat before the make-up bench with her back to the light and her little-child-shoes swinging clear of the ground by six inches. She wriggled herself down to stand looking up at me and then she made me a bobbing little curtsey with one stubby finger under her chin.

"My lord Bothwell!" she exclaimed. "I had forgotten you were such a handsome man."

She walked all around me with her head on one side and surveyed me from every angle.

"I think perhaps you'll do very well as you are," she decided. "I've got a cab waiting at the front door."

She went out of the room before I could open my mouth

and Westlake had obviously been talking to her, for he was standing outside with my heavy cloak across his arm and he draped it over my shoulders, as he did so.

"That'll hide some of your magnificence, my lord."

"I must get changed . . . " I started and Miss Kiddle was out of sight and round the turn in the stairs.

"If you do, you'll lose sight of the little lady," he warned me.

I went down the stairs then two at a time and found her sitting in a taxi, with her hands folded on her lap, as if this was every-day behaviour for her. The taxi driver's eyes nearly fell out of his head, when he saw me, but she surveyed him calmly and told him we were ready to start and in five seconds we had moved out into the traffic and were away. I had wandered into another dream, that was as strange as anything I had dreamt before.

"Where are we going?" I demanded as soon as I had found my voice and even then, I did not recognize it as my own.

"The Old People's Home for Retired Actors and Actresses. It's out at Norton," she remarked, as if we were on a shopping expedition and I had asked the same question and she had answered "Harrod's."

"The Old People's Home . . . I echoed and her voice took on its usual importance, when she discussed the affairs of the Strolling Players.

"We're giving a charity performance there this afternoon. Mr. Mardall is a great friend of the Home . . . a patron, you might say. He agreed to give them some scenes from 'the Merchant' with Ann Perry as Portia. You'll miss that, I'm afraid, but Miss Hemingway is to appear personally afterwards in Mr. Hollidge's adaption of the 'Spanish Lady.' "

"Miss Hemingway . . . " I muttered and she nodded her head and looked down primly at her little hands, still clasped in her lap.

"I thought if you sent in your card, as you wanted to do on another occasion, she might see you afterwards in her dressing room."

I felt that I was in some fearful ante-chamber to disaster and there was no shred of courage in my heart. There was no reality about my present situation and presently, I thought, I should wake up and find myself in my bed in the flat.

"Shouldn't I have changed?" I asked her unhappily in a shaking voice and she looked at me sideways for a moment, before she turned her head to watch the passing traffic.

"You'll do very well as you are, Mr. John," she said and then we sat in silence, for I could think of nothing to say to her and she did not seem to think conversation was necessary.

In a while, we reached the suburb of Norton and a constable on point duty looked at me curiously and then we were past him and off down the High Street. It was a bitterly cold day and there were few people about. Already the evening was drawing down into night and there was more than a hint of snow in the air. The pedestrians walked with shoulders hunched against the weather, their hands in their pockets and their breath condensing in front of their faces in vapour. I wondered if Miss Kiddle could hear my heart thumping against my ribs as we swung through some entrance gates in three minutes and went up a drive through a winter garden of petrified grey grass and desolate rose bushes.

The taxi driver had obviously had instructions where to

go, for he by-passed the front steps of the great flat modern
child's-brick building and stopped outside a side door a
hundred yards along. Miss Kiddle was out of her seat in a
flash and was opening the car door for me and smiling all
over her honest face.

"You do us great honour, Mr. John," she said and took
my hand in hers.

I knew this could not be happening to me in real life. It
had all been a dream . . . Lismore and Juliet and the cottage
on the cliff, the sky and the sea and the gulls.

We went through the door into a little hall and along a
narrow corridor and our footsteps echoed on the bare
boards. Miss Kiddle's finger was at her lips, her voice a
whisper.

"We must be very quiet. The play won't be over yet.
We're early."

We came to the end of the corridor and she led me down
a flight of stone steps and I had quite a task to still the
clattering of my boots and the jingling of the spurs. Then
we rounded a corner and ran straight into Apryl Barldrop.
I got a vivid picture of her against the white-washed wall,
in her black tights and high-necked black sweater, as she
backed away from us towards a door, her eyes wide, her
mouth dropping open.

"Jonathan Harley!" she whispered. "Jonathan Harley!"

Her hand was on the door handle and Miss Kiddle hissed
at her fiercely and took a step forward.

"Don't go through there, Apryl. Have you forgotten
where you are?"

She did not even hear the warning. She opened the door
and backed through it with her eyes still on my face. I took
a stride to the empty doorway and saw that I was in the

wings of a stage. There was a play in progress. Before I could take in the scene, Cedric Barldrop seemed to materialise out of thin air at my side, dressed in his new costume as Bassanio. He watched the backward progress of his sister on to the stage and there was resignation in his face as he glanced back at Miss Kiddle. Then his eyes were raised to the ceiling.

"Oh, gawd!" he muttered. "Now the fat is in the fire. I knew we should have told her about it too."

On stage, Joshua Mardall was rising from an ornate chair of state and I recognized a line from the amended version of "the Spanish Lady", as he ignored Apryl's presence completely.

"And now let's see this great lover of yours," he thundered and Juliet was crouching at his feet with her dark head bent, while Apryl held the centre of the stage, where she had no right whatever to be.

"Jonathan Harley is here," Apryl cried out, "Jonathan Harley himself. I told you he'd come."

Juliet's head jerked to look at her and there was an awful moment of silence. They were caught there in the light from the floats as if they were frozen in time into inanimate statues. There was silence over the whole theatre and then Apryl gasped and spun about to take a horrified look at the audience and another at Bert Hollidge, who was standing at prompt with the book on the ground at his feet.

"Get off stage," he spat out under his breath and Apryl pulled herself together with a visible effort and turned back to where Juliet had risen to her feet. Apryl must have had some vague idea about suiting her words to the period of the play for she took a few hesitant steps in Juliet's direction and said "It's true, my lady. I swear it is. My lord

Bothwell is without. He . . . he . . . he . . . craves an audience with you."

Juliet's eyes swivelled slowly across to meet mine and I thought she was going to faint, for the blood drained away from her face till she looked as if she had been carved from white marble.

"I won't see him," she said. "Send him away. I won't see him."

Apryl was trying to make her way round to the back of the high golden chair to hide herself from Bert Hollidge's scowl.

"Very well, my lady, but he won't go away as easily as all that and I don't blame him after the way you acted last night. You should have seen him then and not behaved so silly."

Old Joshua had taken in the situation and he was nothing, if he was not a good trooper, for his face maintained its calm dignity. Juliet had lost all sense that she was playing to an audience in the tempest of her emotions. She sank down on the chair and bit her nether lip and she had no intention of looking in my direction again. She turned her head to speak to Apryl, who was now safely in the shelter of the chair.

"I never want to see him again."

Joshua was trying to hold the play together against tremendous odds and for a moment I wondered if the whole thing was a put-up job between himself and Miss Kiddle and then I saw that this was not possible. They could not have known they would find me in costume for one thing. I had been supposed to go to her dressing room and see her there. If they had seen fit to tell Apryl of my imminent arrival, the catastrophe would never have occurred.

"I think it might be wiser if we could see this lover of yours," Joshua declared blandly. "We shouldn't let him go away unheard."

Juliet's knuckles were white as she gripped the arms of the chair and the words came stumbling out of her mouth.

"He sent ME away. I went to his house in London . . . weeks before we met him in Scotland, I went there. I told none of you about it. I wanted to ask him to help us. He told his secretary to put me out, he didn't grant me an audience, as you call it. He didn't even care that I over-heard what he said. I was a beggar and I wanted him to pay my debts. That's what he said. I never told anybody about it. I was so ashamed of having gone to him. You all had a high opinion of him, but not I. Long before last night, I knew him for what he was . . . what he is."

Joshua's hand came down on her shoulder as he reasoned with her.

"Don't you think he paid in full for anything he'd done? Don't you think his behaviour over the last few weeks might have been intended as a penance for what he said or did . . . perhaps unintentionally, to offend you?"

Bert Hollidge's prompt came all the way across to me in the doorway, as he gripped his hair in both hands and tried to restore sanity to the stage.

"For God's sake, Juliet, say you'll see him. Let's have a personal appearance of the great Harley and get the bloody tabs down."

She frowned at Hollidge and her voice was like a sulky child's.

"I won't see him. Let him marry his bonnie Queen of Scotland. She'll fit in with his fine ways."

I had thought her very angry with me and perhaps a

little sulky, but her words ended in a sob. There were tears in her eyes and a droop to her mouth and her whole face was mobile with heartbreak. I could bear no more of it. I walked boldly on to the stage with my spurs chinking as I went, I thought I had better behave as if the whole thing was really a play, so I made a deep bow to my lady, as she sat, looking at me blankly and another to Joshua. Joshua smiled at me with warm approval in his eyes and seemed in no way put out that I had barged my way into the scene.

There was a silence over the whole auditorium as the old troopers in their canvas chairs recognized me. I managed to get a look at the front stalls and had taken measure of the house. The theatre was far bigger than I had expected and seemed to consist of the whole basement of the building and there was no doubt in the world that we had a critical audience. They were all old hands at stage-craft and not one of them was under seventy years of age. The men were very flowing in their neckware and dandified in the game way they held their heads. The ladies were gay with ribbons and frills, sparkling with art jewellery and made up to the manner born. Their hearts were warm too as I found out in ten seconds. There was silence, then a gasp of surprise and a whispering of my name. Then they all rose to their feet with a scraping back of chairs. They were clapping and cheering and stamping their feet, but I had put all thought of an audience out of my mind and was down on one knee before my lady with her hand in mine and the jewel on my finger throwing its red fire into my eyes as I bent my head to kiss her fingers.

"Juliet . . . " I pleaded and she tried to pull her hand away from me. I kept it prisoner and thought how strange a thing it was that I was to act out the most important scene of my life upon a stage.

"Have you come to have some more amusement at my expense?" she demanded angrily and I saw a tear run down her cheek and then another. There was misery in the darkness of her eyes before her lashes fanned down to hide it. I knew that the people in the theatre were as unreal to her as they were to me.

"Please listen to me. At least hear what I have to say."

"What do you want with me?"

Her voice was a wraith of its old youth and gaiety and laughter and there was no reality to the bright stage and the pale globed faces in the front rows . . . no more reality in the magnificent figure of old Mardall, nor to the drawn curtains nor to the whole building than there would be to the background of a dream. She was real and I was real and we were alone, face to face in a dramatic scene of tremendous importance to both of us.

"I want you to forgive me for that first day of all, before I even knew you. I want you to understand why I acted as I did in Scotland . . . not telling you, yet it seems that I do nothing but hurt you again and again. I haven't meant to hurt you. I'd rather die than hurt you . . . . "

She tried to be angry with me still but her face was soft and there was love for me in her eyes, like a little flame that would not be put out, as she bit her full lip again and said I had told her a pack of lies. I got to my feet at that and carried the war into her own camp, for I recalled the conversation she had with us in the cottage at Lismore. I walked a little way away from her and then swung back to challenge her.

"Lies?" I demanded. "Lies?"

She nodded her head at me defiantly and I put out an

accusing hand towards her.

"Have you forgotten an evening not so long ago, when you used pretty harsh words about me . . . and with a roomful of witnesses to hear you too . . . when you spoke with the lady, who's now cowering behind your chair? You had no proof of a single thing you said. It was all malicious gossip . . . totally untrue. You took away my character there before them all . . . with lies too . . . every statement you made."

She had the grace to blush at that and I pressed on with my attack.

"I've never loved anybody but you. I told you no lie, when I told you that."

She changed her ground then and went back to her former accusation scornfully.

"You were laughing at me all those weeks. It seems you're not done yet."

"I wasn't laughing at you. I was falling in love with you and you said you loved me. You can't have changed as quickly as that. Can't you forget what's past and let's start afresh? I can't believe . . . . "

She cut across me sharply that she did not want to have any more to do with me.

"Please go away. You're only doing all this so that you can laugh at me . . . and I hate you for it. I hate you for it."

We seemed to have reached an impasse. I looked at her helplessly and wondered what she would do if I took her in my arms and kissed her, but I could find no courage in my heart to do it. The battle was lost, I thought. I had best get myself off the stage with as much grace as I could muster. Then suddenly Cedric was at my side, with a fine sense of timing too, bowing to old Mardall and to Juliet, his face very solemn for the jester's part, that he usually played in life.

"You should be ashamed of yourself," he stormed at her. "I don't know how you can sit there and say he laughed at us. He was kind to us . . . to every one of us. He helped us. My God! How he helped us! Do you think he enjoyed dragging round the country with our measely show, week after week, when he had no obligation to us whatever?"

"Oh, come, my boy!" put in Joshua mildly, but Cedric would not be silenced.

"You'd better know this now, Juliet. We're all with him in this and I can tell you that I, for one, will never speak to you again, if you kick him out without one word of thanks for all he's done for us."

He had been carried along by his emotions, but now he seemed to realize that he was on stage with no excuse in the world and that he would have to reckon with Bert Hollidge afterwards, as indeed we all would. He adapted himself to the costume of Bassanio and took the cloak from my shoulders with a knightly gesture. As he draped it over his arm, the lights made a ruby richness of the crimson lining, that matched my lady's gown. He moved back to stand beside his sister.

"I will have nothing more to do with you," he finished grandly. "If you persist in such cruelty to a noble earl."

"Cruelty?" echoed my lady. "Cruelty?"

I put both hands to my temples in despair at the whole situation.

"Of course you haven't been cruel to me," I said. "I deserve every word you said, but I'm sorry . . . truly sorry. I'll spend the rest of my life making up to you for anything I've done to hurt or offend you."

Her eyes were luminous and soft and I thought she would yield to me soon. I took a step towards her and was halted in my tracks by the entry of Meggie and her husband from the prompt side. Their faces matched each other in grimness but apart from that· they looked an ill-assorted pair. Meggie had snatched up a Spanish shawl from somewhere and had draped it round her shoulders, but this was the only concession she had made to what was supposed to be a period play, for otherwise she wore a good tweed skirt and a hand knitted jumper, a cardigan and a pair of sensible shoes. Sam stumped along half a pace behind in doublet and hose and for good measure carried a pike in his hand.

"For pity's sake, Juliet, stop all these tantrums. If you don't love him, why did you cry all last night and almost make yourself ill?"

Meggie caught the end of the shawl and tossed it impatiently over her shoulder like a scarf, as she went on, "Your grand-father agrees with me about it too. He knew that . . . that my lord Bothwell was coming here today, but he never thought you'd behave the way you've done . . . never."

Sam banged with his pike on the floor and shook his head in disapproval as he caught sight of his two children sheltering behind the golden chair.

"I don't know what young people are coming to these days," he remarked gloomily. "Straight I don't."

Juliet was put out that they were all against her, I think she got a lonely feeling suddenly to see them ranged against her. I think she noticed the subtle feeling that crept out over the whole audience that every last one of them championed my cause and not hers. She covered her face with her hands suddenly and I saw the tears sparkling like diamonds against her fingers and my heart was wrenched with pity for her. I took a step to stand at her side and stroked her bent head gently.

"You invited me to come," I said. "You taught me how to beg and now methinks, you teach me how a beggar should be answered."

She looked up at me at that with the surprise my words gave her and her cheeks were wet with tears.

"I invited you? I did no such thing," she said in a last flash of defiance and I took the ticket out of my sleeve pocket and gave it into her hand. She sat looking down at it, wiping her face with the back of her hand as a small girl might have done . . . and I was miserable that I had vanquished her.

"So?" she whispered and again "So?"

"Please don't send me away. I can't live without you . . . . "

I saw the dreary vista of the years ahead of me if I was to be without her and I would be without her. I had vanquished her but she was too proud to admit defeat. I knelt at her feet and she stood up suddenly and she would have moved away from me too, if I had not clasped her tightly in my arms. I buried my face in the silken folds of her gown and remembered my audience only when I heard the sigh that went up over the whole theatre. I had no shame that they would see me here a beggar at her feet. I must plead my cause with her on the stage, where all my dreams came true.

"I've waited all my life to find you. Don't send me away. For God's sake, have pity on me . . . . "

My face was buried in the crimson folds of her dress

again, so I missed Miss Kiddle's entrance. They told me afterwards that she came on briskly with the dog Toby jumping along at her heels and even the dog was pleading my cause, for he bounced along on his hind legs with his front paws beating the air in appeal. She faced up to Juliet with both hands balled on her hips, her head thrown back, her eyes flashing fire.

"I've no patience with you," she declared sternly. "You've been behaving like a striken moon calf, since the day you set eyes on . . . on . . . on my lord Bothwell here . . . and now you're in a sulk. Yes, my lady. You may think it's a fine demonstration of regal rage, but it's nothing but a fit of the sulks and if I were two feet taller, I'd box your ears."

Joshua Mardall was an old stager. We had all forgotten our audience, but he had not. He stretched out an arm to Miss Kiddle, as he swept the whole company into the wings.

"Let us leave these foolish lovers to their quarrels," he declaimed in a mellifluous voice. "Come, my friends. We will adjourn to the banqueting hall, where presently they will join us, hand in hand. The course of true love . . . . "

He looked back at me as he exited and his merry old eyes twinkled at me.

"Before I go, my lord, I must make you redress. Most humbly I regret that I said it, not once but many times . . . that we would never make an actor out of Mr. John."

So I held the stage with my lady alone at last and there was a feeling of tension over the whole theatre that could not have been surpassed in the greatest drama in the world, but Juliet was not in any theatre. She was alone with me and I was alone with her.

"It's just a play to you," she said flatly. "That's all it ever was."

I had lost control of my voice and the tears were overflowing down my face and still I knelt at her feet.

"If all heaven . . . and the hope of a hereafter . . . and the difference between life . . . and death . . . is a play, then this is a play."

I bent my head to hide the shame of my tears and felt her hand on my hair.

"I'm sorry," she whispered. "I was cruel to you. There was never anything to forgive. My anger was against myself . . . not you. I loved Dandidi. Then Dandidi was the prince. I loved the prince . . . and thought he loved the Queen of Scotland . . . and you mustn't kneel to me. I'm not a great lady. I'm only Juliet."

I got to my feet slowly and took her shoulders between my two hands and remembered how slender she had felt, when I had held her just so in the little theatre in Lismore.

"So you found you loved the prince?"

She clutched the front of my doublet with her hands and cried out that she loved me . . . that she would have died if I hadn't come to her. Then she was in my arms, her head against my shoulder and again, that strange whispering sigh went up through the whole house and recalled me to my situation. Bert Hollidge was glaring at me from the prompt corner and the wings were crowded with the full company. It was high time to bring down the tabs, I thought, for I wanted my lady to myself in the privacy of her dressing room. I bent her backwards and put my lips down on hers and felt the remembered softness of her mouth and the salt taste of her tears. I searched in my mind for a way to close our drama and I thought of the special licence I had to marry her, which was at that moment in Westlake's pocket-book.

"I have a friar waiting to wed us," I smiled at her and held her face between my hands and dared her with my eyes not to carry the play to its close. Her smile was sunshine on a rainy day in spring, when the leaves are in their first green.

"I'll lift you to the back of my white steed and we'll travel fast over the western seas to Tir-nan-oge, for it's a land of happiness, where we'll never grow old with the years . . . and there's an abundance of gold there . . . and much honey and wine . . . . "

Her eyes were very dark blue and the pupils were circles of black velvet softness, as her voice teased me.

"So I was right after all, my lord? Such a land does really exist?"

There was star quality in her, I thought suddenly, for she had that art of throwing the line out to me, as if it were a golden ball and I caught it from her, and threw it back again.

"It exists in the heart of a man, if he has the good fortune to find it."

She put back her head and laughed and I saw that one day, she would stand, as she now stood, on the stage of a great London theatre and take her audience by storm. She would go up across the sky like a rocket, just as I had done myself.

"I can't resist the offer of such a kingdom, if it is my lord's heart . . . especially when his eyes are soft and full of love and his mouth is tender."

She disengaged herself from my arms gracefully and took my hand in hers and then she was down in a curtsey at my feet, with her crimson silk skirt billowing about her on the floor.

"Come, my lord."

The tabs were down at last and we went out to stand at the chalked line on the boards and I wondered what they had made out of our strange drama. Then Joshua Mardall was on and Meggie and Sam, and Apryl and Cedric and last of all, Miss Kiddle came to stand in front of me with the dog Toby at her feet, and I was remembering the day I had met her on the windy shore at Lismore, with a pile of play-bills under her arm . . . and all that had happened since.

The audience was giving us a great reception. They were on their feet again, shouting their approval, so I held up a hand for silence and told them I was to be wed to my lady the next day, though she did not know it yet, and then their delight was something to see. At last the curtain was down and I turned to take her in my arms and kiss her, but there was an interruption once more and this time it was Bert Hollidge. He came stamping out of the prompt corner and his face was as grim as ever I had seen it.

"And now, Mr. Jonathan Harley," he said shortly, "I want a word with you . . . . "